PRAISE FOR ALICE MUNRO

"Alice Munro is not only revered, she is cherished."
—*The New York Review of Books*

"Her work felt revolutionary when I came to it, and it still does."
—Jhumpa Lahiri

"She is one of the handful of writers, some living, most dead, whom I have in mind when I say that fiction is my religion."
—Jonathan Franzen

"A true master of the form."
—Salman Rushdie

"A wonderful writer."
—Joyce Carol Oates

"The authority she brings to the page is just lovely."
—Elizabeth Strout

"She's the most savage writer I've ever read, also the most tender, the most honest, the most perceptive."
—Jeffrey Eugenides

"Alice Munro can move characters through time in a way that no other writer can."
—Julian Barnes

"She is a short-story writer who . . . reimagined what a story can do."
—Lorrie Moore

"There's probably no one alive who's better at the craft of the short story."
—Jim Shepard

ALICE MUNRO
JULIETA

Alice Munro grew up in Wingham, Ontario, and attended the University of Western Ontario. She has published thirteen collections of stories as well as a novel, *Lives of Girls and Women*, and two volumes of *Selected Stories*. During her distinguished career, she has been the recipient of many awards and prizes, including three of Canada's Governor General's Literary Awards and two of its Giller Prizes, the Rea Award for the Short Story, the Lannan Literary Award, England's W. H. Smith Literary Award, the National Book Critics Circle Award, and the Man Booker International Prize. In 2013, she was awarded the Nobel Prize in Literature. Her story "The Bear Came Over the Mountain" was filmed by Sarah Polley as *Away from Her*, and "Hateship, Friendship, Courtship, Loveship, Marriage" as *Hateship Loveship*. She lives in Port Hope, Canada, on Lake Ontario.

ALSO BY ALICE MUNRO

JULIETA

ALICE MUNRO

PENGUIN
an imprint of Penguin Canada,
a division of Penguin Random House Canada Limited

Penguin Canada, 320 Front Street West, Suite 1400, Toronto,
Ontario M5V 3B6, Canada

"Chance," "Soon," and "Silence" originally published in *The New Yorker* on June
14, 2004, first appeared in *Runaway*, originally published in hardcover in Canada by
McClelland and Stewart, and division of Penguin Random House Canada, Toronto,
and in the United States by Alfred A. Knopf, a division of Penguin Random House
LLC, New York, 2004, and subsequently in paperback by Penguin Canada and Vintage
Books in 2005.

Grateful acknowledgment is made to Ludlow Music, Inc., for permission to reprint an
excerpt from the song lyric "Goodnight Irene," words and music by Huddie Ledbetter
and John A. Lomax. TRO-Copyright © 1936 (Renewed), 1950 (Renewed) by Ludlow
Music, Inc., New York, NY. Reprinted by permission of Ludlow Music, Inc.

Manufactured in the U.S.A.

1 2 3 4 5 6 7 8 9 10   (BVG)

Library and Archives Canada Cataloguing in Publication Data is available upon request.

Print ISBN 9780735234239

Book design by Anthea Lingeman

www.penguinrandomhouse.ca

Penguin
Random House
Canada

Contents

Things Within Things

"The complexity of things—the things within things—just seems to be endless. I mean nothing is easy, nothing is simple," Alice Munro said in an interview.

That sentence defines with precision the life and work of the Canadian writer. Simplicity and at the same time denial of that simplicity. Simplicity in order to talk about what is complex, about what happens in front of our eyes without us being able to appreciate at first glance what is extraordinary, bizarre, terrible, grotesque and mysterious about it.

In Alice Munro's stories, nothing is what it seems. Beneath her serene writing there is always something compulsive. Munro has a prodigious ability for finding terrible things within simple things. That ability transforms her into a mistress of suspense. When I read one of her stories, I have to reread it immediately because at the end I have the sensation of knowing less about the story than at the beginning. By means of little hints, comments that arise on the fringes of the main narrative, Munro changes the direction of the story almost without us noticing.

I remember my wonderment and astonishment when I read *Chance*, *Soon* and *Silence*, the three bitter stories from the *Runaway* collection that share Juliet as the protagonist and that made me think that I could take possession of them and turn them into a film. Everything is unpredictable throughout Juliet's life, from her introduction on the train (the 1960s for Alice Munro, which I transferred to the 1980s; sexual emancipation didn't arrive in Spanish society until then) to the solitude of her middle age, abandoned by her daughter without a word of explanation.

Munro's Juliet is a special young woman, cultured and discreet (nothing like the typical thrill seeker), but she has a temperament and a determination capable of making bizarre, reckless decisions. In the first story (*Chance*), Juliet is a young teacher of classical literature who has just finished a period of substitution at the school where she works and she doesn't think twice about going on a long train journey to visit a married man with a sick wife, whom she only knows from having had a chance encounter with him one night on a train journey (Eric, a lobster fisherman who will become the man of her life and the father of her daughter). I don't want to reveal the continuous surprises that await the reader of these three stories, only add that, from those first pages, the character and the unexpected events that she lives through in the following two stories seemed to me to provide precious material for making a film. I began the adaptation by writing everything to do with the train. Putting into practice Munro's idea about the concentration of events in a single place and circumstance (things within things), all the essential elements of the narrative appear in the block of sequences on the night train. On that journey, Juliet comes into contact with the two most important poles of our existence: death and life and, as a consequence, sexual pleasure, the passion of the senses (as the only way to escape from the idea of death), the conception of a new life and the birth of guilt.

Despite the cultural and geographic distance, I have always

felt very close to Alice Munro's themes: the family and family relationships in a rural, provincial or urban setting. And also the desire, the need to escape from all that; always one thing and the opposite, without that meaning the slightest contradiction. Within the family, Munro's specialty is the female characters. Mothers, daughters, sisters, mistresses, friends, grandmothers, housekeepers, neighbors, et cetera. Women with great moral autonomy. Munro is not a complacent writer with her characters, nor is she, I suppose, with her own life, so dear as to provide the title for her latest book (*Dear Life*), the most autobiographical of all.

When Munro talks of her characters' need to abandon the routine in which they live, she uses the terms "escape, hiding and disguise." This drive for escape and concealment is very present in Juliet's three stories. She abandons her sick mother, Sarah, in *Soon*, because that is the natural course of life; a young woman gives priority to the home she has created with a man by whom she already has a daughter, Penelope, rather than to the place where her sick mother is living with a father overflowing with health and desires which he satisfies with another woman who isn't the mother. It's very tough (Munro's stories are always tough) and at the same time something natural but not any less heartrending for that. At the end of *Soon*, for example, we understand Juliet but we also think that she is mean to her mother, however much we empathize with her. At the end of *Silence* it is Juliet who is left on her own: her daughter Penelope goes off to a spiritual retreat and doesn't see her mother again or contact her, except on her birthday, when she sends her a blank card so that she should know that she is still alive but that Juliet is not a part of her life. There is a parallel between these two endings that speaks of the turbulent relationships between mothers and daughters. Also at the end of *Dear Life* Alice Munro reflects on this point in the only way possible: "We say of some things that they can't be forgiven, or that we will never forgive ourselves. But we do—we do it all the time." This reflection can be applied to all three stories.

I found a treasure of inspiration in every line of these three stories, but Munro's style (the best of her, what makes her a writer's writer) is unique and belongs to literature. And even though cinema and literature seem to belong to the same family, they are very different, almost opposing disciplines.

No one should expect *Julieta*, the film, to be the literal translation of these three stories full of magic and pain—it would have been an impossible task—but that doesn't mean my film doesn't depend on them. Julieta exists because previously she was called Juliet and she lived in *Chance*, *Soon* and *Silence*. My *Julieta* is the result of all that links me to Alice Munro (mothers, daughters, fatality, guilt) and of all that separates me, basically our culture and our geography.

Spanish family culture is very different from the North American one. In the United States or Canada, young people become independent when they go to university. In Spain, that is inconceivable; we never completely cut the umbilical cord with our parents. From the moment I decided that I would try to adapt the three stories for the cinema, the first thing I did was unify them, transform them into one story, because in *Runaway* the stories are not consecutive, although they seem to be. Once that was done, I was tempted by the adventure of transforming Juliet into Julieta, that is, transferring Munro's stories to Spain and setting them within our culture and our geography. After several drafts, it seemed that the idea was working. The story of an adaptation is always the story of a betrayal and a pillage, and the case of *Julieta* is no exception.

When I say that cinema and literature are diverse disciplines I don't mean that they don't influence each other mutually. While I was writing the script and directing the film, I clearly saw that Alice Munro's bitter drama demanded from me as a writer and filmmaker a different tone from that which has characterized me until now. I have written many characters of mothers, but Julieta is very different to all of them. For me, Alice Munro's inspiration has meant a real moral, aesthetic and tonal adventure. From the outset, I was fully aware that I had to approach these women in a simple way, that my great adventure would consist of containment and narrative sobriety. Alice Munro's stories asked that of me.

I envy the readers coming to these three stories for the first time. It is a great idea to publish them together and on their own. I am sure that Juliet; her mother, Sarah; her daughter, Penelope; Ailo and Christa are going to accompany you for a long time. The hundred pages or so that their adventures last will multiply in your heart and in your memory like the hypnotic image of the "large wolf crossing the snowy, perfect surface of a small lake" that Juliet contemplates from the train window.

Pedro Almodóvar

JULIETA

CHANCE

———◆———

Halfway through June, in 1965, the term at Torrance House is over. Juliet has not been offered a permanent job—the teacher she replaced has recovered—and she could now be on her way home. But she is taking what she has described as a little detour. A little detour to see a friend who lives up the coast.

About a month ago, she went with another teacher—Juanita, who was the only person on the staff near her age, and her only friend—to see a revival of a movie called *Hiroshima Mon Amour*. Juanita confessed afterwards that she herself, like the woman in the picture, was in love with a married man—the father of a student. Then Juliet said that she had found herself in somewhat the same situation but had not allowed things to go on because of the tragic plight of his wife. His wife was a total invalid, more or less brain-dead. Juanita said that she wished her lover's wife was brain-dead but she was not—she was vigorous and powerful and could get Juanita fired.

And shortly after that, as if conjured by such unworthy lies or half-lies, came a letter. The envelope looked dingy, as if it had spent some time in a pocket, and it was addressed only to "Juliet (Teacher), Torrance House, 1482 Mark St., Vancouver, B.C." The headmistress gave it to Juliet, saying, "I assume this is for you. It's strange there's no surname but they've got the address right. I suppose they could look that up."

Dear Juliet, I forgot which school it was that you're teaching at but the other day I remembered, out of the blue, so it seemed to me a sign that I should write to you. I hope you are still there but the job would have to be pretty awful for you to quit before the term is up and anyway you didn't strike me as a quitter.

How do you like our west coast weather? If you think you have got a lot of rain in Vancouver, then imagine twice as much, and that's what we get up here.

I often think of you sitting up looking at the stairs *stars. You see I wrote stairs, it's late at night and time I was in bed.*

Ann is about the same. When I got back from my trip I thought she had failed a good deal, but that was mostly because I was able to see all at once how she had gone downhill in the last two or three years. I had not noticed her decline when I saw her every day.

I don't think I told you that I was stopping off in Regina to see my son, who is now eleven years old. He lives there with his mother. I noticed a big change in him too.

I'm glad I finally remembered the name of the school but I am awfully afraid now that I can't remember your

*last name. I will seal this anyway and hope the name
comes to me.*

I often think of you.

I often think of you

I often think of you zzzzzz

The bus takes Juliet from downtown Vancouver to Horseshoe
Bay and then onto a ferry. Then across a mainland peninsula
and onto another ferry and onto the mainland again and so
to the town where the man who wrote the letter lives. Whale
Bay. And how quickly—even before Horseshoe Bay—you pass
from city to wilderness. All this term she has been living
amongst the lawns and gardens of Kerrisdale, with the north
shore mountains coming into view like a stage curtain whenever the weather cleared. The grounds of the school were shel-
tered and civilized, enclosed by a stone wall, with something
in bloom at every season of the year. And the grounds of
the houses around it were the same. Such trim abundance—
rhododendrons, holly, laurel, and wisteria. But before you get
even so far as Horseshoe Bay, real forest, not park forest, closes
in. And from then on—water and rocks, dark trees, hanging
moss. Occasionally a trail of smoke from some damp and bat-
tered-looking little house, with a yard full of firewood, lumber
and tires, cars and parts of cars, broken or usable bikes, toys,
all the things that have to sit outside when people are lacking
garages or basements.

The towns where the bus stops are not organized towns at all
In some places a few repetitive houses—company houses—are
built close together, but most of the houses are like those in the
woods, each one in its own wide cluttered yard, as if they have
been built within sight of each other only accidentally. No
paved streets, except the highway that goes through, no side-

walks. No big solid buildings to house Post Offices or Municipal Offices, no ornamented blocks of stores, built to be noticed. No war monuments, drinking fountains, flowery little parks. Sometimes a hotel, which looks as if it is only a pub. Sometimes a modern school or hospital—decent, but low and plain as a shed.

And at some time—noticeably on the second ferry—she begins to have stomach-turning doubts about the whole business.

I often think of you
I think of you often

That is only the sort of thing people say to be comforting, or out of a mild desire to keep somebody on the string.

But there will have to be a hotel, or tourist cabins at least, at Whale Bay. She will go there. She has left her big suitcase at the school, to be picked up later. She has only her travelling bag slung over her shoulder, she won't be conspicuous. She will stay one night. Maybe phone him.

And say what?

That she happens to be up this way to visit a friend. Her friend Juanita, from the school, who has a summer place— where? Juanita has a cabin in the woods, she is a fearless outdoor sort of woman (quite different from the real Juanita, who is seldom out of high heels). And the cabin has turned out to be not far south of Whale Bay. The visit to the cabin and Juanita being over, Juliet has thought—she has thought—since she was nearly there already—she has thought she might as well . . .

Rocks, trees, water, snow. These things, constantly rearranged, made up the scene six months ago, outside the train window on a morning between Christmas and New Year's. The rocks were large, sometimes jutting out, sometimes smoothed like boulders, dark gray or quite black. The trees were mostly evergreens, pine or spruce or cedar. The spruce trees—black spruce—had what looked like little extra trees, miniatures of themselves, stuck right on top. The trees that were not evergreens were spindly and bare—they might be poplar or tamarack or alder. Some of them had spotty trunks. Snow sat in thick caps on top of the rocks and was plastered to the windward side of the trees. It lay in a soft smooth cover over the surface of many big or small frozen lakes. Water was free of ice only in an occasional fast-flowing, dark and narrow stream.

Juliet had a book open on her lap, but she was not reading. She did not take her eyes from what was going by. She was alone in a double seat and there was an empty double seat across from her. This was the space in which her bed was made up at night. The porter was busy in this sleeping car at the moment, dismantling the nighttime arrangements. In some places the dark-green, zippered shrouds still hung down to the floor. There was a smell of that cloth, like tent cloth, and maybe a slight smell of nightclothes and toilets. A blast of fresh winter air whenever anyone opened the doors at either end of the car. The last people were going to breakfast, other people coming back.

There were tracks in the snow, small animal tracks. Strings of beads, looping, vanishing.

Juliet was twenty-one years old and already the possessor of a B.A. and an M.A. in Classics. She was working on her Ph.D. thesis, but had taken time out to teach Latin at a girls' private school in Vancouver. She had no training as a teacher, but an unexpected vacancy at half-term had made the school willing to hire her. Probably no one else had answered the ad. The salary was less than any qualified teacher would be likely to accept. But Juliet was happy to be earning any money at all, after her years on mingy scholarships.

She was a tall girl, fair-skinned and fine-boned, with light-brown hair that even when sprayed did not retain a bouffant style. She had the look of an alert schoolgirl. Head held high, a neat rounded chin, wide thin-lipped mouth, snub nose, bright eyes, and a forehead that was often flushed with effort or appreciation. Her professors were delighted with her—they were grateful these days for anybody who took up ancient languages, and particularly for someone so gifted—but they were worried, as well. The problem was that she was a girl. If she got married—which might happen, as she was not bad-looking for a scholarship girl, she was not bad-looking at all—she would waste all her hard work and theirs, and if she did not get married she would probably become bleak and isolated, losing out on promotions to men (who needed them more, as they had to support families). And she would not be able to defend the oddity of her choice of Classics, to accept what people would see as its irrelevance, or dreariness, to slough that off the way a man could. Odd choices were simply easier for men, most of whom would find women glad to marry them. Not so the other way around.

When the teaching offer came they urged her to take it. Good for you. Get out into the world a bit. See some real life.

Juliet was used to this sort of advice, though disappointed to hear it coming from these men who did not look or sound as if they had knocked about in the real world very eagerly themselves. In the town where she grew up her sort of intelligence was often put in the same category as a limp or an extra thumb, and people had been quick to point out the expected accompanying drawbacks—her inability to run a sewing machine or tie up a neat parcel, or notice that her slip was showing. What would become of her, was the question.

That occurred even to her mother and father, who were proud of her. Her mother wanted her to be popular, and to that end had urged her to learn to skate and to play the piano. She did neither willingly, or well. Her father just wanted her to fit in.

You have to fit in, he told her, otherwise people will make your life hell. (This ignored the fact that he, and particularly Juliet's mother, did not fit in so very well themselves, and were not miserable. Perhaps he doubted Juliet could be so lucky.)

I do, said Juliet once she got away to college. In the Classics Department I fit in. I am extremely okay.

But here came the same message, from her teachers, who had seemed to value and rejoice in her. Their joviality did not hide their concern. Get out into the world, they had said. As if where she had been till now was nowhere.

Nevertheless, on the train, she was happy.

Taiga, she thought. She did not know whether that was the right word for what she was looking at. She might have had, at some level, the idea of herself as a young woman in a Russian novel, going out into an unfamiliar, terrifying, and exhilarating landscape where the wolves would howl at night and where she would meet her fate. She did not care that this fate—in a Russian novel—would likely turn out to be dreary, or tragic, or both.

Personal fate was not the point, anyway. What drew her in— enchanted her, actually— was the very indifference, the repetition, the carelessness and contempt for harmony, to be found on the scrambled surface of the Precambrian shield.

A shadow appeared in the corner of her eye. Then a trousered leg, moving in.

"Is this seat taken?"

Of course it wasn't. What could she say?

Tasselled loafers, tan slacks, tan and brown checked jacket with pencil lines of maroon, dark-blue shirt, maroon tie with flecks of blue and gold. All brand-new and all—except for the shoes—looking slightly too large, as if the body inside had shrunk somewhat since the purchase.

He was a man perhaps in his fifties, with strands of bright

golden-brown hair plastered across his scalp. (It couldn't be dyed, could it, who would dye such a scanty crop of hair?) His eyebrows darker, reddish, peaked and bushy. The skin of his face all rather lumpy, thickened like the surface of sour milk.

Was he ugly? Yes, of course. He was ugly, but so in her opinion were many, many men of around his age. She would not have said, afterwards, that he was remarkably ugly.

His eyebrows went up, his light-colored, leaky eyes widened, as if to project conviviality. He settled down opposite her. He said, "Not much to see out there."

"No." She lowered her eyes to her book.

"Ah," he said, as if things were opening up in a comfortable way. "And how far are you going?"

"Vancouver."

"Me too. All the way across the country. May as well see it all while you're at it, isn't that right?"

"Mm."

But he persisted.

"Did you get on at Toronto too?"

"Yes."

"That's my home, Toronto. I lived there all my life. Your home there too?"

"No," said Juliet, looking at her book again and trying hard to prolong the pause. But something—her upbringing, her embarrassment, God knows perhaps her pity, was too strong for her, and she dealt out the name of her hometown, then placed it for him by giving its distance from various larger towns, its position as regarded Lake Huron, Georgian Bay.

"I've got a cousin in Collingwood. That's nice country, up there. I went up to see her and her family, a couple of times. You travelling on your own? Like me?"

He kept flapping his hands one over the other.

"Yes." No more, she thinks. No more.

"This is the first time I went on a major trip anywhere. Quite a trip, all on your own."

Juliet said nothing.

"I just saw you there reading your book all by yourself and I thought, maybe she's all by herself and got a long way to go too, so maybe we could just sort of chum around together?"

At those words, *chum around*, a cold turbulence rose in Juliet. She understood that he was not trying to pick her up. One of the demoralizing things that sometimes happened was that rather awkward and lonely and unattractive men would make a bald bid for her, implying that she had to be in the same boat as they were. But he wasn't doing that. He wanted a friend, not a girl-friend. He wanted a *chum*.

Juliet knew that, to many people, she might seem to be odd and solitary—and so, in a way, she was. But she had also had the experience, for much of her life, of feeling surrounded by people who wanted to drain away her attention and her time and her soul. And usually, she let them.

Be available, be friendly (especially if you are not *popular*)—that was what you learned in a small town and also in a girls' dormitory. Be accommodating to anybody who wants to suck you dry, even if they know nothing about who you are.

She looked straight at this man and did not smile. He saw her resolve, there was a twitch of alarm in his face.

"Good book you got there? What's it about?"

She was not going to say that it was about ancient Greece and the considerable attachment that the Greeks had to the irrational. She would not be teaching Greek, but was supposed to be teaching a course called Greek Thought, so she was reading Dodds again to see what she could pick up. She said, "I do want to read. I think I'll go to the observation car."

And she got up and walked away, thinking that she shouldn't have said where she was going, it was possible that he might get up and follow her, apologizing, working up to another plea. Also, that it would be cold in the observation car, and she would wish that she had brought her sweater. Impossible to go back now to get it.

The wraparound view from the observation car, at the back of the train, seemed less satisfying to her than the view from the sleeping-car window. There was now always the intrusion of the train itself, in front of you.

Perhaps the problem was that she was cold, just as she had thought she would be. And disturbed. But not sorry. One moment more and his clammy hand would have been proffered—she thought that it would have been either clammy or dry and scaly—names would have been exchanged, she would have been locked in. It was the first victory of this sort that she had ever managed, and it was against the most pitiable, the saddest opponent. She could hear him now, chewing on the words *chum around*. Apology and insolence. Apology his habit. And insolence the result of some hope or determination breaking the surface of his loneliness, his hungry state.

It was necessary but it hadn't been easy, it hadn't been easy at all. In fact it was more of a victory, surely, to stand up to someone in such a state. It was more of a victory than if he had been slick and self-assured. But for a while she would be somewhat miserable.

There were only two other people sitting in the observation car. Two older women, each of them sitting alone. When Juliet saw a large wolf crossing the snowy, perfect surface of a small lake, she knew that they must see it too. But neither broke the silence, and that was pleasing to her. The wolf took no notice of the train, he did not hesitate or hurry. His fur was long, silvery shading into white. Did he think it made him invisible?

While she was watching the wolf, another passenger had arrived. A man, who took the seat across the aisle from hers.

He too carried a book. An elderly couple followed—she small and sprightly, he large and clumsy, taking heavy disparaging breaths.

"Cold up here," he said, when they were settled.

"Do you want me to go get your jacket?"

"Don't bother."

"It's no bother."

"I'll be all right."

In a moment the woman said, "You certainly do get a view here." He did not answer, and she tried again. "You can see all round."

"What there is to see."

"Wait till we go through the mountains. That'll be something. Did you enjoy your breakfast?"

"The eggs were runny."

"I know." The woman commiserated. "I was thinking, I should just have barged into the kitchen and done them myself."

"Galley. They call it a galley."

"I thought that was on a boat."

Juliet and the man across the aisle raised their eyes from their books at the same moment, and their glances met, with a calm withholding of any expression. And in this second or two the train slowed, then stopped, and they looked elsewhere.

They had come to a little settlement in the woods. On the one side was the station, painted a dark red, and on the other a few houses painted the same color. Homes or barracks, for the railway workers. There was an announcement that there would be a stop here for ten minutes.

The station platform had been cleared of snow, and Juliet, peering ahead, saw some people getting off the train to walk about. She would have liked to do this herself, but not without a coat.

The man across the aisle got up and went down the steps

without a look around. Doors opened somewhere below, bringing a stealthy stream of cold air. The elderly husband asked what they were doing here, and what was the name of this place anyway. His wife went to the front of the car to try to see the name, but she was not successful.

Juliet was reading about maenadism. The rituals took place at night, in the middle of winter, Dodds said. The women went up to the top of Mount Parnassus, and when they were, at one time, cut off by a snowstorm, a rescue party had to be sent. The would-be maenads were brought down with their clothes stiff as boards, having, in all their frenzy, accepted rescue. This seemed rather like contemporary behavior to Juliet, it somehow cast a modern light on the celebrants' carrying-on. Would the students see it so? Not likely. They would probably be armed against any possible entertainment, any involvement, as students were. And the ones who weren't so armed wouldn't want to show it.

The call to board sounded, the fresh air was cut off, there were reluctant shunting movements. She raised her eyes to watch, and saw, some distance ahead, the engine disappearing around a curve.

And then a lurch or a shudder, a shudder that seemed to pass along the whole train. A sense, up here, of the car rocking. An abrupt stop.

Everybody sat waiting for the train to start again, and nobody spoke. Even the complaining husband was silent. Minutes passed. Doors were opening and closing. Men's voices calling, a spreading feeling of fright and agitation. In the club car, which was just below, a voice of authority—maybe the conductor's. But it was not possible to hear what he was saying.

Juliet got up and went to the front of the car, looking over the tops of all the cars ahead. She saw some figures running in the snow.

One of the lone women came up and stood beside her.

"I felt there was something going to happen," the woman said. "I felt it back there, when we were stopped. I didn't want us to start up again, I thought something was going to happen."

The other lone woman had come to stand behind them.

"It won't be anything," she said. "Maybe a branch across the tracks."

"They have that thing that goes ahead of the train," the first woman told her. "It goes on purpose to catch things like a branch across the tracks."

"Maybe it had just fallen."

Both women spoke with the same north-of-England accent and without the politeness of strangers or acquaintances. Now that Juliet got a good look at them she saw that they were probably sisters, though one had a younger, broader face. So they travelled together but sat separately. Or perhaps they'd had a row.

The conductor was mounting the stairs to the observation car. He turned, halfway up, to speak.

"Nothing serious to worry about, folks, it seems like we hit an obstacle on the track. We're sorry for the delay and we'll get going again as soon as we can, but we could be here a little while. The steward tells me there's going to be free coffee down here in a few minutes."

Juliet followed him down the stairs. She had become aware, as soon as she stood up, that there was a problem of her own which would make it necessary for her to go back to her seat and her travelling case, whether the man she snubbed was still there or not. As she made her way through the cars she met other people on the move. People were pressing against the windows on one side of the train, or they had halted between the cars, as if they expected the doors to open. Juliet had no time to ask questions, but as she slid past she heard that it might have been a bear, or an elk, or a cow. And people wondered what a cow would be doing up here in the bush, or why the bears were not all asleep now, or if some drunk had fallen asleep on the tracks.

In the dining car people were sitting at the tables, whose white cloths had all been removed. They were drinking the free coffee.

Nobody was in Juliet's seat, or in the seat across from it. She picked up her case and hurried along to the Ladies. Monthly bleeding was the bane of her life. It had even, on occasion, interfered with the writing of important three-hour examinations, because you couldn't leave the room for reinforcements.

Flushed, crampy, feeling a little dizzy and sick, she sank down on the toilet bowl, removed her soaked pad and wrapped it in toilet paper and put it in the receptacle provided. When she stood up she attached the fresh pad from her bag. She saw that the water and urine in the bowl was crimson with her blood. She put her hand on the flush button, then noticed in front of her eyes the warning not to flush the toilet while the train was standing still. That meant, of course, when the train was standing near the station, where the discharge would take place, very disagreeably, right where people could see it. Here, she might risk it.

But just as she touched the button again she heard voices close by, not in the train but outside the toilet window of pebbled glass. Maybe train workers walking past.

She could stay till the train moved, but how long would that be? And what if somebody desperately wanted in? She decided that all she could do was to put down the lid and get out.

She went back to her own seat. Across from her, a child four or five years old was slashing a crayon across the pages of a coloring book. His mother spoke to Juliet about the free coffee.

"It may be free but it looks like you have to go and get it yourself," she said. "Would you mind watching him while I go?"

"I don't want to stay with her," the child said, without looking up.

"I'll go," said Juliet. But at that moment a waiter entered the car with the coffee wagon.

"There. I shouldn't've complained so soon," the mother said. "Did you hear it was a b-o-d-y?"

Juliet shook her head.

"He didn't have a coat on even. Somebody saw him get off and walk on up ahead but they never realized what he was doing. He must've just got round the curve so the engineer couldn't see him till it was too late."

A few seats ahead, on the mother's side of the aisle, a man said, "Here they come back," and some people got up, from Juliet's side, and stooped to see. The child stood up too, pressed his face to the glass. His mother told him to sit down.

"You color. Look at the mess you made, all over the lines."

"I can't look," she said to Juliet. "I can't stand to look at anything like that."

Juliet got up and looked. She saw a small group of men tramping back towards the station. Some had taken off their coats, which were piled on top of the stretcher that a couple of them were carrying.

"You can't see anything," a man behind Juliet said to a woman who had not stood up. "They got him all covered."

Not all of the men who proceeded with their heads lowered were railway employees. Juliet recognized the man who had sat across from her up in the observation car.

After ten or fifteen minutes more, the train began to move. Around the curve there was no blood to be seen, on either side of the car. But there was a trampled area, a shovelled mound of snow. The man behind her was up again. He said, "That's where it happened, I guess," and watched for a little while to see if there was anything else, then turned around and sat down.

The train, instead of speeding to make up for lost time, seemed to be going more slowly than previously. Out of respect, perhaps, or with apprehension about what might lie ahead, around the next curve. The headwaiter went through the car announcing the first seating for lunch, and the mother and child at once got up and followed him. A procession began, and Juliet heard a woman who was passing say, "Really?"

The woman talking to her said softly, "That's what she said. Full of blood. So it must have splashed in when the train went over—"

"Don't say it."

A little later, when the procession had ended and the early lunchers were eating, the man came through—the man from the observation car who had been seen outside walking in the snow.

Juliet got up and quickly pursued him. In the black cold space between the cars, just as he was pushing the heavy door in front of him, she said, "Excuse me. I have to ask you something."

This space was full of sudden noise, the clanking of heavy wheels on the rails.

"What is it?"

"Are you a doctor? Did you see the man who—"

"I'm not a doctor. There's no doctor on the train. But I have some medical experience."

"How old was he?"

The man looked at her with a steady patience and some displeasure.

"Hard to say. Not young."

"Was he wearing a blue shirt? Did he have blondish-brown-colored hair?"

He shook his head, not to answer her question but to refuse it.

"Was this somebody you knew?" he said. "You should tell the conductor if it was."

"I didn't know him."

"Excuse me, then." He pushed open the door and left her.

Of course. He thought she was full of disgusting curiosity, like many other people.

Full of blood. That was disgusting, if you liked.

She could never tell anybody about the mistake that had been made, the horrid joke of it. People would think her exceptionally crude and heartless, were she ever to speak of it. And what was at one end of the misunderstanding—the suicide's smashed body—would seem, in the telling, to be hardly more foul and frightful than her own menstrual blood.

Never tell that to anybody. (Actually she did tell it, a few years later, to a woman named Christa, a woman whose name she did not yet know.)

But she wanted very much to tell somebody something. She got out her notebook and on one of its ruled pages began to write a letter to her parents.

We have not yet reached the Manitoba border and most people have been complaining that the scenery is rather monotonous but they cannot say that the trip has been lacking in dramatic incident. This morning we stopped at some godforsaken little settlement in the northern woods, all painted Dreary Railway Red. I was sitting at the back of the train in the Observation Car, and freezing to death because they skimp on the heat up there (the idea must be that the scenic glories will distract you from your discomfort) and I was too lazy to trudge back and get my sweater. We sat around there for ten or fifteen minutes and then started up again, and I could see

the engine rounding a curve up ahead, and then suddenly
there was a sort of Awful Thump . . .

She and her father and her mother had always made it their
business to bring entertaining stories into the house. This had
required a subtle adjustment not only of the facts but of one's
position in the world. Or so Juliet had found, when her world
was school. She had made herself into a rather superior, invul-
nerable observer. And now that she was away from home all the
time this stance had become habitual, almost a duty.

But as soon as she had written the words *Awful Thump*, she
found herself unable to go on. Unable, in her customary lan-
guage, to go on.

She tried looking out the window, but the scene, composed of
the same elements, had changed. Less than a hundred miles on,
it seemed as if there was a warmer climate. The lakes were
fringed with ice, not covered. The black water, black rocks,
under the wintry clouds, filled the air with darkness. She grew
tired watching, and she picked up her Dodds, opening it just
anywhere, because, after all, she had read it before. Every few
pages she seemed to have had an orgy of underlining. She was
drawn to these passages, but when she read them she found that
what she had pounced on with such satisfaction at one time now
seemed obscure and unsettling.

> *. . . what to the partial vision of the living appears as the*
> *act of a fiend, is perceived by the wider insight of the*
> *dead to be an aspect of cosmic justice . . .*

The book slipped out of her hands, her eyes closed, and she
was now walking with some children (students?) on the surface
of a lake. Everywhere each of them stepped there appeared a

five-sided crack, all of these beautifully even, so that the ice became like a tiled floor. The children asked her the name of these ice tiles, and she answered with confidence, *iambic pentameter*. But they laughed and with this laughter the cracks widened. She realized her mistake then and knew that only the right word would save the situation, but she could not grasp it.

She woke and saw the same man, the man she had followed and pestered between the cars, sitting across from her.

"You were sleeping." He smiled slightly at what he had said. "Obviously."

She had been sleeping with her head hanging forward, like an old woman, and there was a dribble at the corner of her mouth. Also, she knew she must get to the Ladies Toilet at once, hoping there was nothing on her skirt. She said "Excuse me" (just what he had last said to her) and took up her case and walked away with as little self-conscious haste as she could manage.

When she came back, washed and tidied and reinforced, he was still there.

He spoke at once. He said that he wanted to apologize.

"It occurred to me I was rude to you. When you asked me—"

"Yes," she said.

"You had it right," he said. "The way you described him."

This seemed less an offering, on his part, than a direct and necessary transaction. If she did not care to speak he might just get up and walk away, not particularly disappointed, having done what he'd come to do.

Shamefully, Juliet's eyes overflowed with tears. This was so unexpected that she had no time to look away.

"Okay," he said. "It's okay."

She nodded quickly, several times, sniffled wretchedly, blew her nose on the tissue she eventually found in her bag.

"It's all right," she said, and then she told him, in a straightforward way, just what had happened. How the man bent over and asked her if the seat was taken, how he sat down, how she had been looking out the window and how she couldn't do that any longer so she had tried or had pretended to read her book, how he had asked where she had got on the train, and found out where she lived, and kept trying to make headway with the conversation, till she just picked up and left him.

The only thing she did not reveal to him was the expression *chum around*. She had a notion that if she were to say that she would burst into tears all over again.

"People interrupt women," he said. "Easier than men."

"Yes. They do."

"They think women are bound to be nicer."

"But he just wanted somebody to talk to," she said, shifting sides a little. "He wanted somebody worse than I *didn't* want somebody. I realize that now. And I don't look mean. I don't look cruel. But I was."

A pause, while she once more got her sniffling and her leaky eyes under control.

He said, "Haven't you ever wanted to do that to anybody before?"

"*Yes.* But I've never done it. I never have gone so far. And why I did it this time—it was that he was so humble. And he had all new clothes on he'd probably bought for the trip. He was probably depressed and thought he'd go on a trip and it was a good way to meet people and make friends.

"Maybe if he'd just been going a little way—," she said. "But he said he was going to Vancouver and I would have been saddled with him. For days."

"Yes."

"I really might have been."

"Yes."

"So."

"Rotten luck," he said, smiling a very little. "The first time you get up the nerve to give somebody the gears he throws himself under a train."

"It could have been the last straw," she said, now feeling slightly defensive. "It could have been."

"I guess you'll just have to watch out, in future."

Juliet raised her chin and looked at him steadily.

"You mean I'm exaggerating."

Then something happened that was as sudden and unbidden as her tears. Her mouth began to twitch. Unholy laughter was rising.

"I guess it is a little extreme."

He said, "A little."

"You think I'm dramatizing?"

"That's natural."

"But you think it's a mistake," she said, with the laughter under control. "You think feeling guilty is just an indulgence?"

"What I think is——," he said. "I think that this is minor. Things will happen in your life—things will probably happen in your life—that will make this seem minor. Other things you'll be able to feel guilty about."

"Don't people always say that, though? To somebody who is younger? They say, oh, you won't think like this someday. You wait and see. As if you didn't have a right to any serious feelings. As if you weren't capable."

"Feelings," he said. "I was talking about experience."

"But you are sort of saying that guilt isn't any use. People do say that. Is it true?"

"You tell me."

They went on talking about this for a considerable time, in low voices, but so forcefully that people passing by sometimes looked astonished, or even offended, as people may when they overhear debates that seem unnecessarily abstract. Juliet realized, after a while, that though she was arguing—rather well, she thought—for the necessity of some feelings of guilt both in public and in private life, she had stopped feeling any, for the moment. You might even have said that she was enjoying herself.

He suggested that they go forward to the lounge, where they could drink coffee. Once there Juliet discovered that she was quite hungry, though the lunch hours were long over. Pretzels and peanuts were all that could be procured, and she gobbled them up in such a way that the thoughtful, slightly competitive conversation they were having before was not retrievable. So they talked instead about themselves. His name was Eric Porteous, and he lived in a place called Whale Bay, somewhere north of Vancouver, on the west coast. But he was not going there immediately, he was breaking the trip in Regina, to see some people he had not seen for a long time. He was a fisherman, he caught prawns. She asked about the medical experience he had referred to, and he said, "Oh, it's not very extensive. I did some medical study. When you're out in the bush or on the boat anything can happen. To the people you're working with. Or to yourself."

He was married, his wife's name was Ann.

Eight years ago, he said, Ann had been injured in a car accident. For several weeks she was in a coma. She came out of that, but she was still paralyzed, unable to walk or even to feed herself. She seemed to know who he was, and who the woman who looked after her was—with the help of this woman he was able to keep her at home—but her attempts to talk, and to understand what was going on around her, soon faded away.

They had been to a party. She hadn't particularly wanted to go but he had wanted to go. Then she decided to walk home by herself, not being very happy with things at the party.

It was a gang of drunks from another party who ran off the road and knocked her down. Teenagers.

Luckily, he and Ann had no children. Yes, luckily.

"You tell people about it and they feel they have to say, how terrible. What a tragedy. Et cetera."

"Can you blame them?" said Juliet, who had been about to say something of the sort herself.

No, he said. But it was just that the whole thing was a lot more complicated than that. Did Ann feel that it was a tragedy? Probably not. Did he? It was something you got used to, it was a new kind of life. That was all.

All of Juliet's enjoyable experience of men had been in fantasy. One or two movie stars, the lovely tenor—not the virile heartless hero—on a certain old recording of *Don Giovanni*. Henry V, as she read about him in Shakespeare and as Laurence Olivier had played him in the movie.

This was ridiculous, pathetic, but who ever needed to know? In actual life there had been humiliation and disappointment, which she had tried to push out of her mind as quickly as possible.

There was the experience of being stranded head and shoulders above the gaggle of other unwanted girls at the high school dances, and being bored but making a rash attempt to be lively on college dates with boys she didn't much like, who did not much like her. Going out with the visiting nephew of her thesis adviser last year and being broken into—you couldn't call it rape, she too was determined—late at night on the ground in Willis Park.

On the way home he had explained that she wasn't his type. And she had felt too humiliated to retort—or even to be aware, at that moment—that he was not hers.

She had never had fantasies about a particular, real man—

least of all about any of her teachers. Older men—in real life—seemed to her to be slightly unsavory.

This man was how old? He had been married for at least eight years—and perhaps two years, two or three years, more than that. Which made him probably thirty-five or thirty-six. His hair was dark and curly with some gray at the sides, his forehead wide and weathered, his shoulders strong and a little stooped. He was hardly any taller than she was. His eyes were wide set, dark, and eager but also wary. His chin was rounded, dimpled, pugnacious.

She told him about her job, the name of the school— Torrance House. ("What do you want to bet it's called Torments?") She told him that she was not a real teacher but that they were glad to get anybody who had majored in Greek and Latin at college. Hardly anybody did anymore.

"So why did you?"

"Oh, just to be different, I guess."

Then she told him what she had always known that she should never tell any man or boy, lest he lose interest immediately.

"And because I love it. I love all that stuff. I really do."

They ate dinner together—each drinking a glass of wine— and then went up to the observation car, where they sat in the dark, all by themselves. Juliet had brought her sweater this time.

"People must think there's nothing to see up here at night," he said. "But look at the stars you can see on a clear night."

Indeed the night was clear. There was no moon—at least not yet—and the stars appeared in dense thickets, both faint and bright. And like anyone who had lived and worked on boats, he was familiar with the map of the sky. She was able to locate only the Big Dipper.

"That's your start," he said. "Take the two stars on the side of the Dipper opposite the handle. Got them? Those are the pointers. Follow them up. Follow them, you'll find the pole-star." And so on.

He found for her Orion, which he said was the major constellation in the Northern Hemisphere in winter. And Sirius, the Dog Star, at that time of year the brightest star in the whole northern sky.

Juliet was pleased to be instructed but also pleased when it came her turn to be the instructor. He knew the names but not the history.

She told him that Orion was blinded by Enopion but had got his sight back by looking at the sun.

"He was blinded because he was so beautiful, but Hephaestus came to his rescue. Then he was killed anyway, by Artemis, but he got changed into a constellation. It often happened when somebody really valuable got into bad trouble, they were changed into a constellation. Where is Cassiopeia?"

He directed her to a not very obvious W.

"It's supposed to be a woman sitting down."

"That was on account of beauty too," she said.

"Beauty was dangerous?"

"You bet. She was married to the king of Ethiopia and she was the mother of Andromeda. And she bragged about her beauty and for punishment she was banished to the sky. Isn't there an Andromeda, too?"

"That's a galaxy. You should be able to see it tonight. It's the most distant thing you can see with the naked eye."

Even when guiding her, telling her where to look in the sky, he never touched her. Of course not. He was married.

"Who was Andromeda?" he asked her.

"She was chained to a rock but Perseus rescued her."

· · ·

Whale Bay.

A long dock, a number of large boats, a gas station and store that has a sign in the window saying that it is also the bus stop and the Post Office.

A car parked at the side of this store has in its window a homemade taxi sign. She stands just where she stepped down from the bus. The bus pulls away. The taxi toots its horn. The driver gets out and comes towards her.

"All by yourself," he says. "Where are you headed for?"

She asks if there is a place where tourists stay. Obviously there won't be a hotel.

"I don't know if there's anybody renting rooms out this year. I could ask them inside. You don't know anybody around here?"

Nothing to do but to say Eric's name.

"Oh sure," he says with relief. "Hop in, we'll get you there in no time. But it's too bad, you pretty well missed the wake."

At first she thinks that he said *wait*. Or *weight*? She thinks of fishing competitions.

"Sad time," the driver says, now getting in behind the wheel. "Still, she wasn't ever going to get any better."

Wake. The wife. Ann.

"Never mind," he says. "I expect there'll still be some people hanging around. Of course you did miss the funeral. Yesterday. It was a monster. Couldn't get away?"

Juliet says, "No."

"I shouldn't be calling it a wake, should I? Wake is what you have before they're buried, isn't it? I don't know what you call what takes place after. You wouldn't want to call it a party, would you? I can just run you up and show you all the flowers and tributes, okay?"

Inland, off the highway, after a quarter of a mile or so of rough dirt road, is Whale Bay Union Cemetery. And close to the fence is the mound of earth altogether buried in flowers. Faded real flowers, bright artificial flowers, a little wooden cross with the name and date. Tinselly curled ribbons that have blown about all over the cemetery grass. He draws her attention to all the ruts, the mess the wheels of so many cars made yesterday.

"Half of them had never even seen her. But they knew him, so they wanted to come anyway. Everybody knows Eric."

They turn around, drive back, but not all the way back to the highway. She wants to tell the driver that she has changed her mind, she does not want to visit anybody, she wants to wait at the store to catch the bus going the other way. She can say that she really did get the day wrong, and now she is so ashamed of having missed the funeral that she does not want to show up at all.

But she cannot get started. And he will report on her, no matter what.

They are following narrow, winding back roads, past a few houses. Every time they go by a driveway without turning in, there is a feeling of reprieve.

"Well, here's a surprise," the driver says, and now they do turn in. "Where's everybody gone? Half a dozen cars when I drove past an hour ago. Even his truck's gone. Party over. Sorry—I shouldn't've said that."

"If there's nobody here," Juliet says eagerly, "I could just go back down."

"Oh, somebody's here, don't worry about that. Ailo's here. There's her bike. You ever meet Ailo? You know, she's the one took care of things?" He is out and opening her door.

As soon as Juliet steps out, a large yellow dog comes bounding and barking, and a woman calls from the porch of the house.

"Aw go on, Pet," the driver says, pocketing the fare and getting quickly back into the car.

"Shut up. Shut up, Pet. Settle down. She won't hurt you," the woman calls. "She's just a pup."

Pet's being a pup, Juliet thinks, would not make her any less likely to knock you down. And now a small reddish-brown dog arrives to join in the commotion. The woman comes down the steps, yelling, "Pet. Corky. You behave. If they think you are scared of them they will just get after you the worse."

Her *just* sounds something like *chust*.

"I'm not scared," says Juliet, jumping back when the yellow dog's nose roughly rubs her arm.

"Come on in, then. Shut up, the two of you, or I will knock your heads. Did you get the day mixed up for the funeral?"

Juliet shakes her head as if to say that she is sorry. She introduces herself.

"Well, it is too bad. I am Ailo." They shake hands.

Ailo is a tall, broad-shouldered woman with a thick but not flabby body, and yellowish-white hair loose over her shoulders. Her voice is strong and insistent, with some rich production of sounds in the throat. A German, Dutch, Scandinavian accent?

"You better sit down here in the kitchen. Everything is in a mess. I will get you some coffee."

The kitchen is bright, with a skylight in the high, sloping ceiling. Dishes and glasses and pots are piled everywhere. Pet and Corky have followed Ailo meekly into the kitchen, and have started to lap out whatever is in the roasting pan that she has set down on the floor.

Beyond the kitchen, up two broad steps, there is a shaded, cavernous sort of living room, with large cushions flung about on the floor.

Ailo pulls out a chair at the table. "Now sit down. You sit down here and have some coffee and some food."

"I'm fine without," says Juliet.

"No. There is the coffee I have just made, I will drink mine while I work. And there are so much things left over to eat."

She sets before Juliet, with the coffee, a piece of pie—bright green, covered with some shrunken meringue.

"Lime Jell-O," she says, withholding approval. "Maybe it tastes all right, though. Or there is rhubarb?"

Juliet says, "Fine."

"So much mess here. I clean up after the wake, I get it all set-tled. Then the funeral. Now after the funeral I have to clean up all over again."

Her voice is full of sturdy grievance. Juliet feels obliged to say, "When I finish this I can help you."

"No. I don't think so," Ailo says. "I know everything." She is moving around not swiftly but purposefully and effectively. (Such women never want your help. They can tell what you're like.) She continues drying the glasses and plates and cutlery, putting what she has dried away in cupboards and drawers. Then scraping the pots and pans—including the one she retrieves from the dogs—submerging them in fresh soapy water, scrub-bing the surfaces of the table and the counters, wringing the dishcloths as if they were chickens' necks. And speaking to Juliet, with pauses.

"You are a friend of Ann? You know her from before?"

"No."

"No. I think you don't. You are too young. So why do you want to come to her funeral?"

"I didn't," says Juliet. "I didn't know. I just came by to visit." She tries to sound as if this was a whim of hers, as if she had lots of friends and wandered about making casual visits.

With singular fine energy and defiance Ailo polishes a pot, as she chooses not to reply to this. She lets Juliet wait through sev-eral more pots before she speaks.

"You come to visit Eric. You found the right house. Eric lives here."

"You don't live here, do you?" says Juliet, as if this might change the subject.

"No. I do not live here. I live down the hill, with my huss-band." The word *hussband* carries a weight, of pride and reproach.

Without asking, Ailo fills up Juliet's coffee cup, then her own. She brings a piece of pie for herself. It has a rosy layer on the bottom and a creamy layer on top.

"Rhubarb cusstart. It has to be eaten or it will go bad. I do not need it, but I eat it anyway. Maybe I get you a piece?"

"No. Thank you."

"Now. Eric has gone. He will not be back tonight. I do not think so. He has gone to Christa's place. Do you know Christa?"

Juliet tightly shakes her head.

"Here we all live so that we know the other people's situa-tions. We know well. I do not know what it is like where you live. In Vancouver?" (Juliet nods.) "In a city. It is not the same. For Eric to be so good to look after his wife he must need help, do you see? I am one to help him."

Quite unwisely Juliet says, "But do you not get paid?"

"Certain I am paid. But it is more than a job. Also the other kind of help from a woman, he needs that. Do you understand what I am saying? Not a woman with a hussband, I do not believe in that, it is not nice, that is a way to have fights. First Eric had Sandra, then she has moved away and he has Christa. There was a little while both Christa and Sandra, but they were good friends, it was all right. But Sandra has her kids, she wants to move away to bigger schools. Christa is an artist. She makes things out of wood that you find on the beach. What is it you call that wood?"

"Driftwood," says Juliet unwillingly. She is paralyzed by disappointment, by shame.

"That is it. She takes them to places and they sell them for her. Big things. Animals and birds but not realist. Not realist?"

"Not realistic?"

"Yes. Yes. She has never had any children. I don't think she will want to be moving away. Eric has told you this? Would you like more coffee? There is still some in the pot."

"No. No thanks. No he hasn't."

"So. Now I have told you. If you have finish I will take the cup to wash."

She detours to nudge with her shoe the yellow dog lying on the other side of the refrigerator.

"You got to get up. Lazy girl. Soon we are going home.

"There is a bus goes back to Vancouver, it goes through at ten after eight," she says, busy at the sink with her back to the room. "You can come home with me and when it is time my hussband will drive you. You can eat with us. I ride my bike, I ride slow so you can keep up. It is not far."

The immediate future seems set in place so firmly that Juliet gets up without a thought, looks around for her bag. Then she sits down again, but in another chair. This new view of the kitchen seems to give her resolve.

"I think I'll stay here," she says.

"Here?"

"I don't have anything much to carry. I'll walk to the bus."

"How will you know your way? It is a mile."

"That's not far." Juliet wonders about knowing the way, but thinks that, after all, you just have to head downhill.

"He is not coming back, you know," says Ailo. "Not tonight."

"That doesn't matter."

Ailo gives a massive, perhaps disdainful, shrug.

"Get up, Pet. Up." Over her shoulder she says, "Corky stays here. Do you want her in or out?"

"I guess out."

"I will tie her up, then, so she cannot follow. She may not want to stay with a stranger."

Juliet says nothing.

"The door locks when we go out. You see? So if you go out and want to come back in, you have to press this. But when you leave you don't press. It will be locked. Do you understand?"

"Yes."

"We did not use to bother locking here, but now there are too many strangers."

After they had been looking at the stars, the train had stopped for a while in Winnipeg. They got out and walked in a wind so cold that it was painful for them to breathe, let alone speak. When they boarded the train again they sat in the lounge and he ordered brandy.

"Warm us up and put you to sleep," he said.

He was not going to sleep. He would sit up until he got off at Regina, some time towards morning.

Most of the berths were already made up, the dark-green curtains narrowing the aisles, when he walked her back to her car. All the cars had names, and the name of hers was Miramichi.

"This is it," she whispered, in the space between the cars, his hand already pushing the door for her.

"Say good-bye here, then." He withdrew his hand, and they balanced themselves against the jolting so that he could kiss her thoroughly. When that was finished he did not let go, but held her and stroked her back, and then began to kiss her all over her face.

But she pulled away, she said urgently, "I'm a virgin."

"Yes, yes." He laughed, and kissed her neck, then released her and pushed the door open in front of her. They walked down the aisle till she located her own berth. She flattened herself against the curtain, turning, and rather expecting him to kiss her again or touch her, but he slid by almost as if they had met by accident.

How stupid, how disastrous. Afraid, of course, that his stroking hand would go farther down and reach the knot she had made securing the pad to the belt. If she had been the sort of girl who could rely on tampons this need never have happened.

And why *virgin?* When she had gone to such unpleasant lengths, in Willis Park, to insure that such a condition would not be an impediment? She must have been thinking of what she would tell him—she would never be able to tell him that she was menstruating—in the event that he hoped to carry things further. How could he have had plans like that, anyway? How? Where? In her berth, with so little room and all the other passengers very likely still awake around them? Standing up, swaying back and forth, pressed against a door, which anybody could come along and open, in that precarious space between the cars?

So now he could tell someone how he listened all evening to this fool girl showing off what she knew about Greek mythology, and in the end —when he finally kissed her good night, to get rid of her—she started screaming that she was a virgin.

He had not seemed the sort of man to do that, to talk like that, but she could not help imagining it.

She lay awake far into the night, but had fallen asleep when the train stopped at Regina.

. . .

Left alone, Juliet could explore the house. But she does no such thing. It is twenty minutes, at least, before she can be rid of the presence of Ailo. Not that she is afraid that Ailo might come back to check up on her, or to get something she has forgotten. Ailo is not the sort of person who forgets things, even at the end of a strenuous day. And if she had thought Juliet would steal anything, she would simply have kicked her out.

She is, however, the sort of woman who lays claim to space, particularly to kitchen space. Everything within Juliet's gaze speaks of Ailo's occupation, from the potted plants (herbs?) on the windowsill to the chopping block to the polished linoleum.

And when she has managed to push Ailo back, not out of the room but perhaps back beside the old-fashioned refrigerator, Juliet comes up against Christa. Eric has a woman. Of course he has. Christa. Juliet sees a younger, a more seductive Ailo. Wide hips, strong arms, long hair—all blond with no white—breasts bobbing frankly under a loose shirt. The same aggressive— and in Christa, sexy—lack of chic. The same relishing way of chewing up and then spitting out her words.

Two other women come into her mind. Briseis and Chryseis. Those playmates of Achilles and Agamemnon. Each of them described as being "of the lovely cheeks." When the professor read that word (which she could not now remember), his fore- head had gone quite pink and he seemed to be suppressing a giggle. For that moment, Juliet despised him.

So if Christa turns out to be a rougher, more northerly ver- sion of Briseis/Chryseis, will Juliet be able to start despising Eric as well?

But how will she ever know, if she walks down to the high- way and gets on the bus?

The fact is that she never intended to get on that bus. So it seems. With Ailo out of the way, it is easier to discover her own intentions. She gets up at last and makes more coffee, then pours it into a mug, not one of the cups that Ailo has put out.

She is too keyed up to be hungry, but she examines the bottles on the counter, which people must have brought for the wake. Cherry brandy, peach schnapps, Tia Maria, sweet vermouth. These bottles have been opened but the contents have not proved popular. The serious drinking has been done from the empty bottles ranged by Ailo beside the door. Gin and whisky, beer and wine.

She pours Tia Maria into her coffee, and takes the bottle with her up the steps into the big living room.

This is one of the longest days of the year. But the trees around here, the big bushy evergreens and the red-limbed arbutus, shut out the light from the descending sun. The skylight keeps the kitchen bright, while the windows in the living room are nothing but long slits in the wall, and there the darkness has already begun to accumulate. The floor is not finished—old shabby rugs are laid down on squares of plywood—and the room is oddly and haphazardly furnished. Mostly with cushions, lying about on the floor, a couple of hassocks covered in leather, which has split. A huge leather chair, of the sort that leans back and has a rest for your feet. A couch covered by an authentic but ragged patchwork quilt, an ancient television set, and brick-and-plank bookshelves—on which there are no books, only stacks of old *National Geographic*s, with a few sailing magazines and issues of *Popular Mechanics*.

Ailo obviously has not got around to cleaning up this room. There are smudges of ashes where ashtrays have been upset onto the rugs. And crumbs everywhere. It occurs to Juliet that she might look for the vacuum cleaner, if there is one, but then she thinks that even if she could get it to work it is likely that some mishap would occur—the thin rugs might get scrunched up and caught in the machine, for instance. So she just sits in the leather chair, adding more Tia Maria as the level of her coffee goes down.

Nothing is much to her liking on this coast. The trees are too large and crowded together and do not have any personality of their own—they simply make a forest. The mountains are too grand and implausible and the islands that float upon the waters of the Strait of Georgia are too persistently picturesque. This house, with its big spaces and slanted ceilings and unfinished wood, is stark and self-conscious.

The dog barks from time to time, but not urgently. Maybe she wants to come in and have company. But Juliet has never had a dog—a dog in the house would be a witness, not a companion, and would only make her feel uncomfortable.

Perhaps the dog is barking at exploring deer, or a bear, or a cougar. There has been something in the Vancouver papers about a cougar—she thinks it was on this coast—mauling a child.

Who would want to live where you have to share every part of outdoor space with hostile and marauding animals?

Kallipareos. Of the lovely cheeks. Now she has it. The Homeric word is sparkling on her hook. And beyond that she is suddenly aware of all her Greek vocabulary, of everything which seems to have been put in a closet for nearly six months now. Because she was not teaching Greek, she put it away.

That is what happens. You put it away for a little while, and now and again you look in the closet for something else and you remember, and you think, *soon.* Then it becomes something that is just there, in the closet, and other things get crowded in front of it and on top of it and finally you don't think about it at all.

The thing that was your bright treasure. You don't think about it. A loss you could not contemplate at one time, and now it becomes something you can barely remember.

That is what happens.

And even if it's not put away, even if you make your living from it, every day? Juliet thinks of the older teachers at the school, how little most of them care for whatever it is that they teach. Take Juanita, who chose Spanish because it goes with her Christian name (she is Irish) and who wants to speak it well, to use it in her travels. You cannot say that Spanish is her treasure.

Few people, very few, have a treasure, and if you do you must hang on to it. You must not let yourself be waylaid, and have it taken from you.

The Tia Maria has worked in a certain way with the coffee. It makes her feel careless, but powerful. It enables her to think that Eric, after all, is not so important. He is someone she might dally with. Dally is the word. As Aphrodite did, with Anchises. And then one morning she will slip away.

She gets up and finds the bathroom, then comes back and lies down on the couch with the quilt over her—too sleepy to notice Corky's hairs on it, or Corky's smell.

When she wakes it is full morning, though only twenty past six by the kitchen clock.

She has a headache. There is a bottle of aspirin in the bathroom—she takes two, and washes herself and combs her hair and gets her toothbrush from her bag and brushes her teeth. Then she makes a fresh pot of coffee and eats a slice of home-made bread without bothering to heat or butter it. She sits at the kitchen table. Sunlight, slipping down through the trees, makes coppery splashes on the smooth trunks of the arbutus. Corky begins to bark, and barks for quite a long time before the truck turns into the yard and silences her.

Juliet hears the door of the truck close, she hears him speaking to the dog, and dread comes over her. She wants to hide somewhere (she says later, *I could have crawled under the table*, but of course she does not think of doing anything so ridiculous). It's like the moment at school before the winner of the prize is announced. Only worse, because she has no reasonable hope. And because there will never be another chance so momentous in her life.

When the door opens she cannot look up. On her knees the fingers of both hands are interwoven, clenched together.

"You're here," he says. He is laughing in triumph and admiration, as if at a most spectacular piece of impudence and daring. When he opens his arms it's as if a wind has blown into the room and made her look up.

Six months ago she did not know this man existed. Six months ago, the man who died under the train was still alive, and perhaps picking out the clothes for his trip.

"You're here."

She can tell by his voice that he is claiming her. She stands up, quite numb, and sees that he is older, heavier, more impetuous than she has remembered. He advances on her and she feels herself ransacked from top to bottom, flooded with relief, assaulted by happiness. How astonishing this is. How close to dismay.

It turns out that Eric was not taken so much by surprise as he pretended. Ailo phoned him last night, to warn him about the strange girl, Juliet, and offered to check for him as to whether the girl had got on the bus. He had thought it somehow right to take the chance that she would do so—to test fate, maybe—but when Ailo phoned to say that the girl had not gone he was startled by the joy he felt. Still, he did not come home right away, and he did not tell Christa, though he knew he would have to tell her, very soon.

All this Juliet absorbs bit by bit in the weeks and months that follow. Some information arrives accidentally, and some as the result of her imprudent probing.

Her own revelation (of nonvirginity) is considered minor.

Christa is nothing like Ailo. She does not have wide hips or blond hair. She is a dark-haired, thin woman, witty and sometimes morose, who will become Juliet's great friend and mainstay during the years ahead—though she will never quite forgo a habit of sly teasing, the ironic flicker of a submerged rivalry.

SOON

❖

Two profiles face each other. One the profile of a pure white heifer, with a particularly mild and tender expression, the other that of a green-faced man who is neither young nor old. He seems to be a minor official, maybe a postman—he wears that sort of cap. His lips are pale, the whites of his eyes shining. A hand that is probably his offers up, from the lower margin of the painting, a little tree or an exuberant branch, fruited with jewels.

At the upper margin of the painting are dark clouds, and underneath them some small tottery houses and a toy church with its toy cross, perched on the curved surface of the earth. Within this curve a small man (drawn to a larger scale, however, than the buildings) walks along purposefully with a scythe on his shoulder, and a woman, drawn to the same scale, seems to wait for him. But she is hanging upside down.

There are other things as well. For instance, a girl milking a cow, within the heifer's cheek.

Juliet decided at once to buy this print for her parents' Christmas present.

"Because it reminds me of them," she said to Christa, her friend who had come down with her from Whale Bay to do some shopping. They were in the gift shop of the Vancouver Art Gallery.

Christa laughed. "The green man and the cow? They'll be flattered."

Christa never took anything seriously at first, she had to make some joke about it. Juliet wasn't bothered. Three months pregnant with the baby that would turn out to be Penelope, she was suddenly free of nausea, and for that reason, or some other, she was subject to fits of euphoria. She thought of food all the time, and hadn't even wanted to come into the gift shop, because she had spotted a lunchroom.

She loved everything in the picture, but particularly the little figures and rickety buildings at the top of it. The man with the scythe and the woman hanging upside down.

She looked for the title. *I and the Village.*

It made exquisite sense.

"Chagall. I like Chagall," said Christa. "Picasso was a bastard."

Juliet was so happy with what she had found that she could hardly pay attention.

"You know what he is supposed to have said? *Chagall is for shopgirls,*" Christa told her. "So what's wrong with shopgirls? Chagall should have said, Picasso is for people with funny faces."

"I mean, it makes me think of their life," Juliet said. "I don't know why, but it does."

She had already told Christa some things about her

parents—how they lived in a curious but not unhappy isolation, though her father was a popular schoolteacher. Partly they were cut off by Sara's heart trouble, but also by their subscribing to magazines nobody around them read, listening to programs on the national radio network, which nobody around them listened to. By Sara's making her own clothes—sometimes ineptly—from *Vogue* patterns, instead of Butterick. Even by the way they preserved some impression of youth instead of thickening and slouching like the parents of Juliet's schoolfellows. Juliet had described Sam as looking like her—long neck, a slight bump to the chin, light-brown floppy hair—and Sara as a frail pale blonde, a wispy untidy beauty.

When Penelope was thirteen months old, Juliet flew with her to Toronto, then caught the train. This was in 1969. She got off in a town twenty miles or so away from the town where she had grown up, and where Sam and Sara still lived. Apparently the train did not stop there anymore.

She was disappointed to get off at this unfamiliar station and not to see reappear, at once, the trees and sidewalks and houses she remembered—then, very soon, her own house, Sam and Sara's house, spacious but plain, no doubt with its same blistered and shabby white paint, behind its bountiful soft-maple tree.

Sam and Sara, here in this town where she'd never seen them before, were smiling but anxious, diminished.

Sara gave a curious little cry, as if something had pecked her. A couple of people on the platform turned to look.

Apparently it was only excitement.

"We're long and short, but still we match," she said.

At first Juliet did not understand what was meant. Then she figured it out—Sara was wearing a black linen skirt down to her calves and a matching jacket. The jacket's collar and cuffs were of a shiny lime-green cloth with black polka dots. A turban of the same green material covered her hair. She must have made the outfit herself, or got some dressmaker to make it for her. Its colors were unkind to her skin, which looked as if fine chalk dust had settled over it.

Juliet was wearing a black minidress.

"I was wondering what you'd think of me, black in the summertime, like I'm all in mourning," Sara said. "And here you're dressed to match. You look so smart, I'm all in favor of these short dresses."

"And long hair," said Sam. "An absolute hippy." He bent to look into the baby's face. "Hello, Penelope."

Sara said, "What a dolly."

She reached out for Penelope—though the arms that slid out of her sleeves were sticks too frail to hold any such burden. And they did not have to, because Penelope, who had tensed at the first sound of her grandmother's voice, now yelped and turned away, and hid her face in Juliet's neck.

Sara laughed. "Am I such a scarecrow?" Again her voice was ill controlled, rising to shrill peaks and falling away, drawing stares. This was new—though maybe not entirely. Juliet had an idea that people might always have looked her mother's way when she laughed or talked, but in the old days it would have been a spurt of merriment they noticed, something girlish and attractive (though not everybody would have liked that either, they would have said she was always trying to get attention).

Juliet said, "She's so tired."

Sam introduced the young woman who was standing behind them, keeping her distance as if she was taking care not to be identified as part of their group. And in fact it had not occurred to Juliet that she was.

"Juliet, this is Irene. Irene Avery."

Juliet stuck out her hand as well as she could while holding

Penelope and the diaper bag, and when it became evident that Irene was not going to shake hands—or perhaps did not notice the intention—she smiled. Irene did not smile back. She stood quite still but gave the impression of wanting to bolt.

"Hello," said Juliet.

Irene said, "Pleased to meet you," in a sufficiently audible voice, but without expression.

"Irene is our good fairy," Sara said, and then Irene's face did change. She scowled a little, with sensible embarrassment.

She was not as tall as Juliet—who was tall—but she was broader in the shoulders and hips, with strong arms and a stubborn chin. She had thick, springy black hair, pulled back from her face into a stubby ponytail, thick and rather hostile black eyebrows, and the sort of skin that browns easily. Her eyes were green or blue, a light surprising color against this skin, and hard to look into, being deep set. Also because she held her head slightly lowered and twisted her face to the side. This wariness seemed hardened and deliberate.

"She does one heck of a lot of work for a fairy," Sam said, with his large strategic grin. "I'll tell the world she does."

And now of course Juliet recalled the mention in letters of some woman who had come in to help, because of Sara's strength having gone so drastically downhill. But she had thought of somebody much older. Irene was surely no older than she was herself.

The car was the same Pontiac that Sam had got secondhand maybe ten years ago. The original blue paint showed in streaks here and there but was mostly faded to gray, and the effects of winter road salt could be seen in its petticoat fringe of rust.

"The old gray mare," said Sara, almost out of breath after the short walk from the railway platform.

"She hasn't given up," said Juliet. She spoke admiringly, as seemed to be expected. She had forgotten that this was what they called the car, though it was the name she had thought up herself.

"Oh, she never gives up," said Sara, once she was settled with Irene's help in the backseat. "And we'd never give up on her."

Juliet got into the front seat, juggling Penelope, who was beginning again to whimper. The heat inside the car was shocking, even though it had been parked with the windows down in the scanty shade of the station poplars.

"Actually I'm considering——," said Sam as he backed out, "I'm considering turning her in for a truck."

"He doesn't mean it," shrieked Sara.

"For the business," Sam continued. "It'd be a lot handier. And you'd get a certain amount of advertising every time you drove down the street, just from the name on the door."

"He's teasing," Sara said. "How am I going to ride around in a vehicle that says *Fresh Vegetables?* Am I supposed to be the squash or the cabbage?"

"Better pipe down, Missus," Sam said, "or you won't have any breath left when we reach home."

After nearly thirty years of teaching in the public schools around the county— -ten years in the last school—Sam had suddenly quit and decided to get into the business of selling vegetables, full-time. He had always cultivated a big vegetable garden, and raspberry canes, in the extra lot beside their house, and they had sold their surplus produce to a few people around town. But now, apparently, this was to change into his way of making a living, selling to grocery stores and perhaps eventually putting up a market stall at the front gate.

"You're serious about all this?" said Juliet quietly.

"Darn right I am."

"You're not going to miss teaching?"

"Not on your Nelly-O. I was fed up. I was fed up to the eyeballs."

It was true that after all those years, he had never been offered, in any school, the job of principal. She supposed that was what he was fed up with. He was a remarkable teacher, the one whose antics and energy everyone would remember, his Grade Six unlike any other year in his pupils' lives. Yet he had been passed over, time and again, and probably for that very reason. His methods could be seen to undercut authority. So you could imagine Authority saying that he was not the sort of man to be in charge, he'd do less harm where he was.

He liked outdoor work, he was good at talking to people, he would probably do well, selling vegetables.

But Sara would hate it.

Juliet did not like it either. If there was a side to be on, however, she would have to choose his. She was not going to define herself as a snob.

And the truth was that she saw herself—she saw herself and Sam and Sara, but particularly herself and Sam—as superior in their own way to everybody around them. So what should his peddling vegetables matter?

Sam spoke now in a quieter, conspiratorial voice.

"What's her name?"

He meant the baby's.

"Penelope. We're never going to call her Penny. Penelope."

"No, I mean—I mean her last name."

"Oh. Well, it's Henderson-Porteous I guess. Or Porteous-Henderson. But maybe that's too much of a mouthful, when she's already called Penelope? We knew that but we wanted Penelope. We'll have to settle it somehow."

"So. He's given her his name," Sam said. "Well, that's something. I mean, that's good."

Juliet was surprised for a moment, then not.

"Of course he has," she said. Pretending to be mystified and amused. "She's his."

"Oh yes. Yes. But given the circumstances."

"I forget about the circumstances," she said. "If you mean the fact that we're not married, it's hardly anything to take into account. Where we live, the people we know, it is not a thing anybody thinks about."

"Suppose not," said Sam. "Was he married to the first one?"

Juliet had told them about Eric's wife, whom he had cared for during the eight years that she had lived after her car accident.

"Ann? Yes. Well, I don't really know. But yes. I think so. Yes."

Sara called into the front seat, "Wouldn't it be nice to stop for ice cream?"

"We've got ice cream in the fridge at home," Sam called back. And added quietly, shockingly, to Juliet, "Take her into anyplace for a treat, and she'll put on a show."

The windows were still down, the warm wind blew through the car. It was full summer— -a season which never arrived, as far as Juliet could see, on the west coast. The hardwood trees were humped over the far edge of the fields, making blue-black caves of shade, and the crops and the meadows in front of them, under the hard sunlight, were gold and green. Vigorous young wheat and barley and corn and beans—fairly blistering your eyes.

Sara said, "What's this conference in aid of? In the front seat? We can't hear back here for the wind."

Sam said, "Nothing interesting. Just asking Juliet if her fellow's still doing the fishing."

Eric made his living prawn fishing, and had done so for a long time. Once he had been a medical student. That had come to an end because he had performed an abortion, on a friend (not a girlfriend). All had gone well, but somehow the story got out. This was something Juliet had thought of revealing to her broad-minded parents. She had wanted, perhaps, to establish him as an educated man, not just a fisherman. But why should that matter, especially now that Sam was a vegetable man? Also, their broad-mindedness was possibly not so reliable as she had thought.

There was more to be sold than fresh vegetables and berries. Jam, bottled juice, relish, were turned out in the kitchen. The first morning of Juliet's visit, raspberry-jam making was in progress. Irene was in charge, her blouse wet with steam or sweat, sticking to her skin between the shoulder blades. Every so often she flashed a look at the television set, which had been wheeled down the back hall to the kitchen doorway, so that you had to squeeze around it to get into the room. On the screen was a children's morning program, showing a Bullwinkle cartoon. Now and then Irene gave a loud laugh at the cartoon antics, and Juliet laughed a little, to be comradely. Of this Irene took no notice.

Counter space had to be cleared so that Juliet could boil and mash an egg for Penelope's breakfast, and make some coffee and toast for herself. "Is that enough room?" Irene asked her, in a voice that was dubious, as if Juliet was an intruder whose demands could not be foreseen.

Close-up, you could see how many fine black hairs grew on Irene's forearms. Some grew on her cheeks, too, just in front of her ears.

In her sidelong way she watched everything Juliet did, watched her fiddle with the knobs on the stove (not remembering at first which burners they controlled), watched her lifting the egg out of the saucepan and peeling off the shell (which stuck, this time, and came away in little bits rather than in large easy pieces), then watched her choosing the saucer to mash it in.

"You don't want her to drop that on the floor." This was a

reference to the china saucer. "Don't you got a plastic dish for her?"

"I'll watch it," Juliet said.

It turned out that Irene was a mother, too. She had a boy three years old and a daughter just under two. Their names were Trevor and Tracy. Their father had been killed last summer in an accident at the chicken barn where he worked. She herself was three years younger than Juliet—twenty-two. The information about the children and the husband came out in answer to Juliet's questions, and the age could be figured from what she said next.

When Juliet said, "Oh, I'm sorry"—speaking about the accident and feeling that she had been rude to pry, and that it was now hypocritical of her to commiserate—Irene said, "Yeah. Right in time for my twenty-first birthday," as if misfortunes were something to accumulate, like charms on a bracelet.

After Penelope had eaten all of the egg that she would accept, Juliet hoisted her onto one hip and carried her upstairs.

Halfway up she realized that she had not washed the saucer.

There was nowhere to leave the baby, who was not yet walking but could crawl very quickly. Certainly she could not be left for even five minutes in the kitchen, with the boiling water in the sterilizer and the hot jam and the chopping knives—it was too much to ask Irene to watch her. And first thing this morning she had again refused to make friends with Sara. So Juliet carried her up the enclosed stairs to the attic—having shut the door behind—and set her there on the steps to play, while she herself looked for the old playpen. Fortunately Penelope was an expert on steps.

The house was a full two stories tall, its rooms high-ceilinged but boxlike—or so they seemed to Juliet now. The roof was steeply pitched, so that you could walk around in the middle of the attic. Juliet used to do that, when she was a child.

She walked around telling herself some story she had read, with certain additions or alterations. Dancing—that too—in front of an imaginary audience. The real audience consisted of broken or simply banished furniture, old trunks, an immensely heavy buffalo coat, the purple martin house (a present from long-ago students of Sam's, which had failed to attract any purple martins), the German helmet supposed to have been brought home by Sam's father from the First World War, and an unintentionally comic amateur painting of the *Empress of Ireland* sinking in the Gulf of St. Lawrence, with matchstick figures flying off in all directions.

And there, leaning against the wall, was *I and the Village*. Face out—no attempt had been made to hide it. And no dust on it to speak of, so it had not been there long.

She found the playpen, after a few moments of searching. It was a handsome heavy piece of furniture, with a wooden floor and spindle sides. And the baby carriage. Her parents had kept everything, had hoped for another child. There had been one miscarriage at least. Laughter in their bed, on Sunday mornings, had made Juliet feel as if the house had been invaded by a stealthy, even shameful, disturbance, not favorable to herself.

The baby carriage was of the kind that folded down to become a stroller. This was something Juliet had forgotten about, or hadn't known. Sweating by now, and covered with dust, she got to work to effect this transformation. This sort of job was never easy for her, she never grasped right away the manner in which things were put together, and she might have dragged the whole thing downstairs and gone out to the garden to get Sam to help her, but for the thought of Irene. Irene's flickering pale eyes, indirect but measuring looks, competent hands. Her vigilance, in which there was something that couldn't quite be called contempt. Juliet didn't know what it could be called. An attitude, indifferent but uncompromising, like a cat's.

She managed at last to get the stroller into shape. It was cumbersome, half again as big as the stroller she was used to. And filthy, of course. As she was herself by now, and Penelope, on the steps, even more so. And right beside the baby's hand was something Juliet hadn't even noticed. A nail. The sort of thing you paid no attention to, till you had a baby at the hand-to-mouth stage, and that you had then to be on the lookout for all the time.

And she hadn't been. Everything here distracted her. The heat, Irene, the things that were familiar and the things that were unfamiliar.

I and the Village.

"Oh," said Sara. "I hoped you wouldn't notice. Don't take it to heart."

The sunroom was now Sara's bedroom. Bamboo shades had been hung on all the windows, filling the small room—once part of the verandah—with a brownish-yellow light and a uniform heat. Sara, however, was wearing woolly pink pajamas. Yesterday, at the station, with her pencilled eyebrows and raspberry lipstick, her turban and suit, she had looked to Juliet like an elderly Frenchwoman (not that Juliet had seen many elderly Frenchwomen), but now, with her white hair flying out in wisps, her bright eyes anxious under nearly nonexistent brows, she looked more like an oddly aged child. She was sitting up against the pillows with the quilts pulled up to her waist. When Juliet had walked her to the bathroom, earlier, it had been revealed that in spite of the heat she was wearing both socks and slippers in bed.

A straight-backed chair had been placed by her bed, its seat being easier for her to reach than a table. On it were pills and medicines, talcum powder, moisturizing lotion, a half-drunk cup of milky tea, a glass filmed with the traces of some dark tonic, probably iron. On top of the bed were magazines—old copies of *Vogue* and the *Ladies' Home Journal*.

"I'm not," said Juliet.

"We did have it hanging up. It was in the back hall by the dining-room door. Then Daddy took it down."

"Why?"

"He didn't say anything about it to me. He didn't say that he was going to. Then came a day when it was just gone."

"Why would he take it down?"

"Oh. It would be some notion he had, you know."

"What sort of a notion?"

"Oh. I think—you know, I think it probably had to do with Irene. That it would disturb Irene."

"There wasn't anybody naked in it. Not like the Botticelli."

For indeed there was a print of *The Birth of Venus* hanging in Sam and Sara's living room. It had been the subject of nervous jokes years ago on the occasion when they had the other teachers to supper.

"No. But it was *modern*. I think it made Daddy uncomfortable. Or maybe looking at it with Irene looking at it—that made him uncomfortable. He might be afraid it would make her feel—oh, sort of contemptuous of us. You know—that we were weird. He wouldn't like for Irene to think we were that kind of people."

Juliet said, "The kind of people who would hang that kind of picture? You mean he'd care so much what she thought of our *pictures?*"

"You know Daddy."

"He's not afraid to disagree with people. Wasn't that the trouble in his job?"

"What?" said Sara. "Oh. Yes. He can disagree. But he's careful sometimes. And Irene. Irene is—he's careful of her. She's very valuable to us, Irene."

"Did he think she'd quit her job because she thought we had a weird picture?"

"I would have left it up, dear. I value anything that comes from you. But Daddy . . ."

Juliet said nothing. From the time when she was nine or ten until she was perhaps fourteen, she and Sara had an understanding about Sam. *You know Daddy.*

That was the time of their being women together. Home permanents were tried on Juliet's stubborn fine hair, dressmaking sessions produced the outfits like nobody else's, suppers were peanut-butter-and-tomato-and-mayonnaise sandwiches on the evenings Sam stayed late for a school meeting. Stories were told and retold about Sara's old boyfriends and girlfriends, the jokes they played and the fun they had, in the days when Sara was a schoolteacher too, before her heart got too bad. Stories from the time before that, when she lay in bed with rheumatic fever and had the imaginary friends Rollo and Maxine who solved mysteries, even murders, like the characters in certain children's books. Glimpses of Sam's besotted courtship, disasters with the borrowed car, the time he showed up at Sara's door disguised as a tramp.

Sara and Juliet, making fudge and threading ribbons through the eyelet trim on their petticoats, the two of them intertwined. And then abruptly, Juliet hadn't wanted any more of it, she had wanted instead to talk to Sam late at night in the kitchen, to ask him about black holes, the Ice Age, God. She hated the way Sara undermined their talk with wide-eyed ingenuous questions, the way Sara always tried somehow to bring the subject back to herself. That was why the talks had to be late at night and there had to be the understanding neither she nor Sam ever spoke about. *Wait till we're rid of Sara.* Just for the time being, of course.

There was a reminder going along with that. *Be nice to Sara. She risked her life to have you, that's worth remembering.*

"Daddy doesn't mind disagreeing with people that are *over* him," Sara said, taking a deep breath. "But you know how he is with people that are *under* him. He'll do anything to make sure they don't feel he's any different from them, he just has to put himself down on their level—"

Juliet did know, of course. She knew the way Sam talked to the boy at the gas pumps, the way he joked in the hardware store. But she said nothing.

"He has to suck up to them," said Sara with a sudden change of tone, a wavering edge of viciousness, a weak chuckle.

Juliet cleaned up the stroller, and Penelope, and herself, and set off on a walk into town. She had the excuse that she needed a certain brand of mild disinfectant soap with which to wash the diapers—if she used ordinary soap the baby would get a rash. But she had other reasons, irresistible though embarrassing.

This was the way she had walked to school for years of her life. Even when she was going to college, and came home on a visit, she was still the same—a girl going to school. Would she never be done going to school? Somebody asked Sam that at a time when she had just won the Intercollegiate Latin Translation Prize, and he had said, " 'Fraid not." He told this story on himself. God forbid that he should mention prizes. Leave Sara to do that—though Sara might have forgotten just what the prize was for.

And here she was, redeemed. Like any other young woman, pushing her baby. Concerned about the diaper soap. And this wasn't just her baby. Her love child. She sometimes spoke of Penelope that way, just to Eric. He took it as a joke, she said it as a joke, because of course they lived together and had done so for some time, and they intended to go on together. The fact that they were not married meant nothing to him, so far as she knew, and she often forgot about it, herself. But occasionally—and now, especially, here at home, it was the fact of her unmarried state that gave her some flush of accomplishment, a silly surge of bliss.

"So—you went upstreet today," Sam said. (Had he always said *upstreet*? Sara and Juliet said *uptown*.) "See anybody you knew?"

"I had to go to the drugstore," Juliet said. "So I was talking to Charlie Little."

This conversation took place in the kitchen, after eleven o'clock at night. Juliet had decided that this was the best time to make up Penelope's bottles for tomorrow.

"Little Charlie?" said Sam—who had always had this other habit she hadn't remembered, the habit of continuing to call people by their school nicknames. "Did he admire the offspring?"

"Of course."

"And well he might."

Sam was sitting at the table, drinking rye and smoking a cigarette. His drinking whisky was new. Because Sara's father had been a drunk—not a down-and-out drunk, he had continued to practice as a veterinarian, but enough of a terror around the house to make his daughter horrified by drinking—Sam had never used to so much as drink a beer, at least to Juliet's knowledge, at home.

Juliet had gone into the drugstore because that was the only place to buy the diaper soap. She hadn't expected to see Charlie, though it was his family's store. The last she had heard of him, he was going to be an engineer. She had mentioned that to him, today, maybe tactlessly, but he had been easy and jovial when he told her that it hadn't worked out. He had put on weight around the middle, and his hair had thinned, had lost some of its wave and glisten. He had greeted Juliet with enthusiasm, with flattery for herself as well as her baby, and this had confused her, so that she had felt her face and neck hot, slightly perspiring, all the time he talked to her. In high school he would have had no time for her—except for a decent greeting, since his manners were always affable, democratic. He took out the most desirable girls in the school, and was now, as he told her, married to one of them. Janey Peel. They had two children, one of them about Penelope's age, one older. That was the reason, he said, with a candor that seemed to owe something to Juliet's own situation—that was the reason he hadn't gone on to become an engineer.

So he knew how to win a smile and a gurgle from Penelope, and he chatted with Juliet as a fellow parent, somebody now on the same level. She felt idiotically flattered and pleased. But there was more to his attention than that—the quick glance at her unadorned left hand, the joke about his own marriage. And something else. He appraised her, covertly, perhaps he saw her now as a woman displaying the fruits of a boldly sexual life. Juliet, of all people. The gawk, the scholar.

"Does she look like you?" he had asked, when he squatted down to peer at Penelope.

"More like her father," said Juliet casually, but with a flood of pride, the sweat now pearling on her upper lip.

"Does she?" said Charlie, and straightened up, speaking confidentially. "I'll tell you one thing, though. I thought it was a shame—"

. . .

Juliet said to Sam, "He told me he thought it was a shame what happened with you."

"He did, did he? What did you say to that?"

"I didn't know what to say. I didn't know what he meant. But I didn't want him to know that."

"No."

She sat down at the table. "I'd like a drink but I don't like whisky."

"So you drink now, too?"

"Wine. We make our own wine. Everybody in the Bay does."

He told her a joke then, the sort of joke that he would never have told her before. It involved a couple going to a motel, and it ended up with the line "So it's like what I always tell the girls at Sunday school—you don't have to drink and smoke to have a good time."

She laughed but felt her face go hot, as with Charlie.

"Why did you quit your job?" she said. "Were you let go because of me?"

"Come on now." Sam laughed. "Don't think you're so important. I wasn't let go. I wasn't fired."

"All right then. You quit."

"I quit."

"Did it have anything at all to do with me?"

"I quit because I got goddamn sick of my neck always in that noose. I was on the point of quitting for years."

"It had nothing to do with me?"

"All right," Sam said. "I got into an argument. There were things said."

"What things?"

"You don't need to know.

"And don't worry," he said after a moment. "They didn't fire me. They couldn't have fired me. There are rules. It's like I told you—I was ready to go anyway."

"But you don't realize," said Juliet. "You don't *realize*. You don't realize just how *stupid* this is and what a disgusting place this is to live in, where people say that kind of thing, and how if I told people I know this, they wouldn't believe it. It would seem like a joke."

"Well. Unfortunately your mother and I don't live where you live. Here is where we live. Does that fellow of yours think it's a joke too? I don't want to talk any more about this tonight, I'm going to bed. I'm going to look in on Mother and then I'm going to bed."

"The passenger train—," said Juliet with continued energy, even scorn. "It does still stop here. Doesn't it? You didn't want me getting off here. *Did you?*"

On his way out of the room, her father did not answer.

Light from the last streetlight in town now fell across Juliet's bed. The big soft maple tree had been cut down, replaced by a patch of Sam's rhubarb. Last night she had left the curtains closed to shade the bed, but tonight she felt that she needed the outside air. So she had to switch the pillow down to the foot of the bed, along with Penelope, who had slept like an angel with the full light in her face.

She wished she had drunk a little of the whisky. She lay stiff with frustration and anger, composing in her head a letter to Eric. *I don't know what I'm doing here, I should never have come here, I can't wait to go home.*

Home.

. . .

When it was barely light in the morning, she woke to the noise of a vacuum cleaner. Then a voice—Sam's—interrupted this noise, and she must have fallen asleep again. When she woke up later, she thought it must have been a dream. Otherwise Penelope would have woken up, and she hadn't.

The kitchen was cooler this morning, no longer full of the smell of simmering fruit. Irene was fixing little caps of gingham cloth, and labels, onto all the jars.

"I thought I heard you vacuuming," said Juliet, dredging up cheerfulness. "I must have dreamed it. It was only about five o'clock in the morning."

Irene did not answer for a moment. She was writing on a label. She wrote with great concentration, her lips caught between her teeth.

"That was her," she said when she had finished. "She woke your dad up and he had to go and make her quit."

This seemed unlikely. Yesterday Sara had left her bed only to go to the bathroom.

"He told me," said Irene. "She wakes up in the middle of the night and thinks she's going to do something and then he has to get up and make her quit."

"She must have a spurt of energy then," said Juliet.

"Yeah." Irene was getting to work on another label. When that was done, she faced Juliet.

"Wants to wake your dad up and get attention, that's it. Him dead tired and he's got to get out of bed and tend to her."

Juliet turned away. Not wanting to set Penelope down—as if the child wasn't safe here—she juggled her on one hip while she fished the egg out with a spoon, tapped and shelled and mashed it with one hand.

While she fed Penelope she was afraid to speak, lest the tone of her voice alarm the baby and set her wailing. Something communicated itself to Irene, however. She said in a more subdued voice—but with an undertone of defiance—"That's just the way they get. When they're sick like that, they can't help it. They can't think about nobody but themselves."

Sara's eyes were closed, but she opened them immediately. "Oh, my dear ones," she said, as if laughing at herself. "My Juliet. My Penelope."

Penelope seemed to be getting used to her. At least she did not cry, this morning, or turn her face away.

"Here," said Sara, reaching for one of her magazines. "Set her down and let her work at this."

Penelope looked dubious for a moment, then grabbed a page and tore it vigorously.

"There you go," said Sara. "All babies love to tear up magazines. I remember."

On the bedside chair there was a bowl of Cream of Wheat, barely touched.

"You didn't eat your breakfast?" Juliet said. "Is that not what you wanted?"

Sara looked at the bowl as if serious consideration was called for, but couldn't be managed.

"I don't remember. No, I guess I didn't want it." She had a little fit of giggling and gasping. "Who knows? Crossed my mind—she could be poisoning me.

"I'm just kidding," she said when she recovered. "But she's very fierce. Irene. We mustn't underestimate—Irene. Did you see the hairs on her arms?"

"Like cats' hairs," said Juliet.

"Like skunks'."

"We must hope none of them get into the jam."

"Don't make me—laugh any more—"

Penelope became so absorbed in tearing up magazines that in

a while Juliet was able to leave her in Sara's room and carry the Cream of Wheat out to the kitchen. Without saying anything, she began to make an eggnog. Irene was in and out, carrying boxes of jam jars to the car. On the back steps, Sam was hosing off the earth that clung to the newly dug potatoes. He had begun to sing—too softly at first for his words to be heard. Then, as Irene came up the steps, more loudly.

> *"Irene, good ni-i-ight,*
> *Irene, good night,*
> *Good night, Irene, good night, Irene,*
> *I'll see you in my dreams."*

Irene, in the kitchen, swung around and yelled, "Don't sing that song about me."

"What song about you?" said Sam, with feigned amazement. "Who's singing a song about you?"

"You were. You just were."

"Oh—that song. That song about Irene? The girl in the song? By golly—I forgot that was your name too."

He started up again, but humming, stealthily. Irene stood listening, flushed, with her chest going up and down, waiting to pounce if she should hear a word.

"Don't you sing about me. If it's got my name in it, it's about me."

Suddenly Sam burst out in full force.

> *"Last Saturday night I got married,*
> *Me and my wife settled down—"*

"Stop it. You stop it," cried Irene, wide-eyed, inflamed. "If you don't stop I'll go out there and squirt the hose on you."

. . .

Sam was delivering jam, that afternoon, to various grocery stores and a few gift shops which had placed orders. He invited Juliet to come along. He had gone to the hardware store and bought a brand-new baby's car seat for Penelope.

"That's one thing we don't have in the attic," he said. "When you were little, I don't know if they had them. Anyway, it wouldn't have mattered. We didn't have a car."

"It's very spiffy," said Juliet. "I hope it didn't cost a fortune."

"A mere bagatelle," said Sam, bowing her into the car.

Irene was in the field picking more raspberries. These would be for pies. Sam tooted the horn twice and waved as they set off, and Irene decided to respond, raising one arm as if batting away a fly.

"That's a dandy girl," Sam said. "I don't know how we would have survived without her. But I imagine she seems pretty rough to you."

"I hardly know her."

"No. She's scared stiff of you."

"Surely not." And trying to think of something appreciative or at least neutral to say about Irene, Juliet asked how her husband had been killed at the chicken barn.

"I don't know if he was a criminal type or just immature. Anyway, he got in with some goons who were planning a sideline in stolen chickens and of course they managed to set off the alarm and the farmer came out with a gun and whether he meant to shoot him or not he did—"

"My God."

"So Irene and her in-laws went to court but the fellow got off. Well, he would. It must have been pretty hard on her, though. Even if it doesn't seem that the husband was much of a prize."

Juliet said that of course it must have been, and asked him if Irene was somebody he had taught at school.

"No no no. She hardly got to school, as far as I can make out."

He said that her family had lived up north, somewhere near Huntsville. Yes. Somewhere near there. One day they all went into town. Father, mother, kids. And the father told them he had things to do and he would meet them in a while. He told them where. When. And they walked around with no money to spend, until it was time. And he just never showed up.

"Never intended to show up. Ditched them. So they had to go on welfare. Lived in some shack out in the country, where it was cheap. Irene's older sister, the one who was the mainstay, more than the mother, I gather—she died of a burst appendix. No way of getting her into town, snowstorm on and they didn't have a phone. Irene didn't want to go back to school then, because her sister had sort of protected her from the way the other kids would act towards them. She may seem thick-skinned now but I guess she wasn't always. Maybe even now it's more of a masquerade."

And now, he said, now Irene's mother was looking after the little boy and the little girl, but guess what, after all these years the father had shown up and was trying to get the mother to go back to him, and if that should happen Irene didn't know what she'd do, since she didn't want her kids near him.

"They're cute kids, too. The little girl has some problem with a cleft palate and she's already had one operation but she'll need another later on. She'll be all right. But that's just one more thing."

One more thing.

What was the matter with Juliet? She felt no real sympathy. She felt herself rebelling, deep down, against this wretched litany. It was too much. When the cleft palate appeared in the story what she had really wanted to do was complain. *Too much.*

She knew she was wrong, but the feeling would not budge. She was afraid to say anything more, lest out of her mouth she betray her hard heart. She was afraid she would say to Sam, "Just what is so wonderful about all this misery, does it make her a saint?" Or she might say, most unforgivably, "I hope you don't mean to get us mixed up with people like that."

"I'm telling you," Sam said, "at the time she came to help us out I was at wits' end. Last fall, your mother was a downright catastrophe. And not exactly that she was letting everything go. No. Better if she had let everything go. Better if she'd done nothing. What she did, she'd start one job up and then she could not get on with it. Over and over. Not that this was anything absolutely new. I mean, I always had to pick up after her and look after her and help her do the housework. Me and you both—remember? She'd always been this sweet pretty girl with a bad heart and she was used to being waited on. Once in a while over the years it did occur to me she could have tried harder.

"But it got so bad," he said. "It got so I'd come home to the washing machine in the middle of the kitchen floor and wet clothes slopping all over the place. And some baking mess she'd started on and given up on, stuff charred to a crisp in the oven. I was scared she'd set herself on fire. Set the house on fire. I'd tell her and tell her, stay in bed. But she wouldn't and then she'd be all in this mess, crying. I tried a couple of girls coming in and they just couldn't handle her. So then—Irene.

"Irene," he said with a robust sigh. "I bless the day. I tell you. Bless the day."

But like all good things, he said, this must come to an end. Irene was getting married. To a forty- or fifty-year-old widower. Farmer. He was supposed to have money and for her sake Sam guessed he hoped it was true. Because the man did not have much else to recommend him.

"By Jesus he doesn't. As far as I can see he's only got one tooth in his head. Bad sign, in my opinion. Too proud or stingy to get choppers. Think of it—a grand-looking girl like her."

"When is the event?"

"In the fall sometime. In the fall."

Penelope had been sleeping all this time—she had gone to sleep in her car seat almost as soon as they started to move. The front windows were down and Juliet could smell the hay, which was freshly cut and baled—nobody made hay coils anymore. Some elm trees were still standing, marvels now, in their isolation.

They stopped in a village built all along one street in a narrow valley. Bedrock stuck out of the valley walls—the only place for many miles around where such massive rocks were to be seen. Juliet remembered coming here when there was a special park which you paid to enter. In the park there was a fountain, a teahouse where they served strawberry shortcake and ice cream—and surely other things which she could not remember. Caves in the rock were named after each of the Seven Dwarfs. Sam and Sara had sat on the ground by the fountain eating ice cream while she had rushed ahead to explore the caves. (Which were nothing much, really—quite shallow.) She had wanted them to come with her but Sam had said, "You know your mother can't climb."

"You run," Sara had said. "Come back and tell us all about it." She was dressed up. A black taffeta skirt that spread in a circle around her on the grass. Those were called ballerina skirts.

It must have been a special day.

Juliet asked Sam about this when he came out of the store. At first he could not remember. Then he did. A gyp joint, he said. He didn't know when it had disappeared.

Juliet could see no trace anywhere along the street of a fountain or a teahouse.

"A bringer of peace and order," Sam said, and it took a moment for her to recognize that he was still talking about Irene. "She'll turn her hand to anything. Cut the grass and hoe the garden. Whatever she's doing she gives it her best and she behaves as if it's a privilege to do it. That's what never ceases to amaze me."

What could the carefree occasion have been? A birthday, a wedding anniversary?

Sam spoke insistently, even solemnly, over the noise of the car's struggle up the hill.

"She restored my faith in women."

Sam charged into every store after telling Juliet that he wouldn't be a minute, and came back to the car quite a while later explaining that he had not been able to get away. People wanted to talk, people had been saving up jokes to tell him. A few followed him out to see his daughter and her baby.

"So that's the girl who talks Latin," one woman said.

"Getting a bit rusty nowadays," Sam said. "Nowadays she has her hands full."

"I bet," the woman said, craning to get a look at Penelope. "But aren't they a blessing? Oh, the wee ones."

Juliet had thought she might talk to Sam about the thesis she was planning to return to—though at present that was just a dream. Such subjects used to come up naturally between them. Not with Sara. Sara would say, "Now, you must tell me what you're doing in your studies," and Juliet would sum things up, and Sara might ask her how she kept all those Greek names straight. But Sam had known what she was talking about. At college she had mentioned how her father had explained to her what *thaumaturgy* meant, when she ran across the word at the age of twelve or thirteen. She was asked if her father was a scholar.

"Sure," she said. "He teaches Grade Six."

Now she had a feeling that he would subtly try to undermine her. Or maybe not so subtly. He might use the word *airy-fairy*. Or claim to have forgotten things she could not believe he had forgotten.

But maybe he had. Rooms in his mind closed up, the windows blackened—what was in there judged by him to be too useless, too discreditable, to meet the light of day.

Juliet spoke out more harshly than she intended.

"Does she want to get married? Irene?"

This question startled Sam, coming as it did in that tone and after a considerable silence.

"I don't know," he said.

And after a moment, "I don't see how she could."

"Ask her," Juliet said. "You must want to, the way you feel about her."

They drove for a mile or two before he spoke. It was clear she had given offense.

"I don't know what you're talking about," he said.

"Happy, Grumpy, Dopey, Sleepy, Sneezy," Sara said.

"Doc," said Juliet.

"Doc. *Doc.* Happy, Sneezy, *Doc,* Grumpy, *Bashful,* Sneezy— No. Sneezy, Bashful, Doc, Grumpy—*Sleepy,* Happy, Doc, Bashful—"

Having counted on her fingers, Sara said, "Wasn't that eight?

"We went there more than once," she said. "We used to call it the Shrine of Strawberry Shortcake—oh, how I'd like to go again."

"Well, there's nothing there," Juliet said. "I couldn't even see where it was."

"I'm sure I could have. Why didn't I go with you? A summer drive. What strength does it take to ride in a car? Daddy's always saying I haven't the strength."

"You came to meet me."

"Yes I did," said Sara. "But he didn't want me to. I had to throw a fit."

She reached around to pull up the pillows behind her head, but she could not manage it, so Juliet did it for her.

"Drat," said Sara. "What a useless piece of goods I am. I think I could handle a bath, though. What if company comes?"

Juliet asked if she was expecting anybody.

"No. But what if?"

So Juliet took her into the bathroom and Penelope crawled after them. Then when the water was ready and her grandmother hoisted in, Penelope decided that the bath must be for her as well. Juliet undressed her, and the baby and the old woman were bathed together. Though Sara, naked, did not look like an old woman as much as an old girl—a girl, say, who had suffered some exotic, wasting, desiccating disease.

Penelope accepted her presence without alarm, but kept a firm hold on her own duck-shaped yellow soap.

It was in the bath that Sara finally brought herself to ask, circumspectly, about Eric.

"I'm sure he is a nice man," she said.

"Sometimes," said Juliet casually.

"He was so good to his first wife."

"Only wife," Juliet corrected her. "So far."

"But I'm sure now you have this baby—you're happy, I mean. I'm sure you're happy."

"As happy as is consistent with living in sin," Juliet said, surprising her mother by wringing out a dripping washcloth over her soaped head.

"That's what I mean," said Sara after ducking and covering her face, with a joyful shriek. Then, "Juliet?"

"Yes?"

"You know I don't mean it if I ever say mean things about Daddy. I know he loves me. He's just unhappy."

Juliet dreamed she was a child again and in this house, though the arrangement of the rooms was somewhat different. She looked out the window of one of the unfamiliar rooms, and saw an arc of water sparkling in the air. This water came from the hose. Her father, with his back to her, was watering the garden. A figure moved in and out among the raspberry canes and was revealed, after a while, to be Irene—though a more childish Irene, supple and merry. She was dodging the water sprinkled from the hose. Hiding, reappearing, mostly successful but always caught again for an instant before she ran away. The game was supposed to be lighthearted, but Juliet, behind the window, watched it with disgust. Her father always kept his back to her, yet she believed—she somehow *saw*—that he held the hose low, in front of his body, and that it was only the nozzle of it that he turned back and forth.

The dream was suffused with a sticky horror. Not the kind of horror that jostles its shapes outside your skin, but the kind that curls through the narrowest passages of your blood

When she woke that feeling was still with her. She found the dream shameful. Obvious, banal. A dirty indulgence of her own.

. . .

There was a knock on the front door in the middle of the afternoon. Nobody used the front door—Juliet found it a bit stiff to open.

The man who stood there wore a well-pressed yellow shirt with short sleeves, and tan pants. He was perhaps a few years older than she was, tall but rather frail-looking, slightly hollow-chested, but vigorous in his greeting, relentless in his smiling.

"I've come to see the lady of the house," he said.

Juliet left him standing there and went into the sunroom.

"There's a man at the door," she said. "He might be selling something. Should I get rid of him?"

Sara was pushing herself up. "No, no," she said breathlessly. "Tidy me a bit, can you? I heard his voice. It's Don. It's my friend Don."

Don had already entered the house and was heard outside the sunroom door.

"No fuss, Sara. It's only me. Are you decent?"

Sara, with a wild and happy look, reached for the hairbrush she could not manage, then gave up and ran her fingers through her hair. Her voice rang out gaily. "I'm as decent as I'll ever be, I'm afraid. Come in here."

The man appeared, hurried up to her, and she lifted her arms to him. "You smell of summer," she said. "What is it?" She fingered his shirt. "Ironing. Ironed cotton. My, that's nice."

"I did it myself," he said. "Sally's over at the church messing about with the flowers. Not a bad job, eh?"

"Lovely," said Sara. "But you almost didn't get in. Juliet thought you were a salesman. Juliet's my daughter. My dear daughter. I told you, didn't I? I told you she was coming. Don is my minister, Juliet. My friend and minister."

Don straightened up, grasped Juliet's hand.

"Good you're here—I'm very glad to meet you. And you weren't so far wrong, actually. I am a sort of salesman."

Juliet smiled politely at the ministerial joke.

"What church are you the minister of?"

The question made Sara laugh. "Oh dear—that gives the show away, doesn't it?"

"I'm from Trinity," said Don, with his unfazed smile. "And as for giving the show away—it's no news to me that Sara and Sam were not involved with any of the churches in the community. I just started dropping in anyway, because your mother is such a charming lady."

Juliet could not remember whether it was the Anglican or United Church that was called Trinity.

"Would you get Don a reasonable sort of chair, dear?" said Sara. "Here he is bending over me like a stork. And some sort of refreshment, Don? Would you like an eggnog? Juliet makes me the most delicious eggnogs. No. No, that's probably too heavy. You've just come in from the heat of the day. Tea? That's hot too. Ginger ale? Some kind of juice? What juice do we have, Juliet?"

Don said, "I don't need anything but a glass of water. That would be welcome."

"No tea? Really?" Sara was quite out of breath. "But I think I'd like some. You could drink half a cup, surely. Juliet?"

In the kitchen, by herself—Irene could be seen in the garden, today she was hoeing around the beans—Juliet wondered if the tea was a ruse to get her out of the room for a few private words. A few private words, perhaps even a few words of prayer? The notion sickened her.

Sam and Sara had never belonged to any church, though Sam had told someone, early in their life here, that they were Druids. Word had gone around that they belonged to a church not represented in town, and that information had moved them up a notch from having no religion at all. Juliet herself had gone to Sunday school for a while at the Anglican Church, though that was mostly because she had an Anglican friend. Sam, at school, had never rebelled at having to read the Bible and say the Lord's Prayer every morning, any more than he objected to "God Save the Queen."

"There's times for sticking your neck out and times not to," he had said. "You satisfy them this way, maybe you can get away with telling the kids a few facts about evolution."

Sara had at one time been interested in the Baha'i faith, but Juliet believed that this interest had waned.

She made enough tea for the three of them and found some digestive biscuits in the cupboard—also the brass tray which Sara had usually taken out for fancy occasions.

Don accepted a cup, and gulped down the ice water which she had remembered to bring him, but shook his head at the cookies.

"Not for me, thanks."

He seemed to say this with special emphasis. As if godliness forbade him.

He asked Juliet where she lived, what was the nature of the weather on the west coast, what work her husband did.

"He's a prawn fisherman, but he's actually not my husband," said Juliet pleasantly.

Don nodded. Ah, yes.

"Rough seas out there?"

"Sometimes."

"Whale Bay. I've never heard of it but now I'll remember it. What church do you go to in Whale Bay?"

"We don't go. We don't go to church."

"Is there not a church of your sort handy?"

Smiling, Juliet shook her head.

"There *is* no church of our sort. We don't believe in God."

Don's cup made a little clatter as he set it down in its saucer. He said he was sorry to hear that.

"Truly sorry to hear that. How long have you been of this opinion?"

"I don't know. Ever since I gave it any serious thought."

"And your mother's told me you have a child. You have a little girl, don't you?"

Juliet said yes, she had.

"And she has never been christened? You intend to bring her up a heathen?"

Juliet said that she expected Penelope would make up her own mind about that, someday.

"But we intend to bring her up without religion. Yes."

"That is sad," said Don quietly. "For yourselves, it's sad. You and your—whatever you call him—you've decided to reject God's grace. Well. You are adults. But to reject it for your child—it's like denying her nourishment."

Juliet felt her composure cracking. "But we don't *believe*," she said. "We don't believe in God's grace. It's not like denying her nourishment, it's refusing to bring her up on lies."

"Lies. What millions of people all over the world believe in, you call lies. Don't you think that's a little presumptuous of you, calling God a lie?"

"Millions of people don't believe it, they just go to church," said Juliet, her voice heating. "They just don't think. If there is a God, then God gave me a mind, and didn't he intend me to use it?

"Also," she said, trying to hold herself steady "Also, millions of people believe something different. They believe in Buddha, for instance. So how does millions of people believing in anything make it true?"

"Christ is alive," said Don readily. "Buddha isn't."

"That's just something to say. What does it mean? I don't see any proof of either one being alive, as far as that goes."

"*You* don't. But others do. Do you know that Henry Ford— Henry Ford the second, who has everything anybody in life could desire—nevertheless he gets down on his knees and prays to God every night of his life?"

"Henry Ford?" cried Juliet. "Henry Ford? What does anything *Henry Ford* does matter to me?"

The argument was taking the course that arguments of this sort are bound to take. The minister's voice, which had started out more sorrowful than angry—though always indicating iron-clad conviction—was taking on a shrill and scolding tone, while Juliet, who had begun, as she thought, in reasonable resistance— calm, shrewd, rather maddeningly polite—was now in a cold and biting rage. Both of them cast around for arguments and refutations that would be more insulting than useful.

Meanwhile Sara nibbled on a digestive biscuit, not looking up at them. Now and then she shivered, as if their words struck her, but they were beyond noticing.

What did bring their display to an end was the loud wailing of Penelope, who had wakened wet and had complained softly for a while, then complained more vigorously, and finally given way to fury. Sara heard her first, and tried to attract their attention.

"Penelope," she said faintly, then, with more effort, "Juliet. Penelope." Juliet and the minister both looked at her distract-edly, and then the minister said, with a sudden drop in his voice, "Your baby."

Juliet hurried from the room. She was shaking when she picked Penelope up, she came close to stabbing her when she was pinning on the dry diaper. Penelope stopped crying, not because she was comforted but because she was alarmed by this

rough attention. Her wide wet eyes, her astonished stare, broke
into Juliet's preoccupation, and she tried to settle herself down,
talking as gently as she could and then picking her child up,
walking with her up and down the upstairs hall. Penelope was
not immediately reassured, but after a few minutes the tension
began to leave her body.

Juliet felt the same thing happening to her, and when she
thought that a certain amount of control and quiet had returned
to both of them, she carried Penelope downstairs.

The minister had come out of Sara's room and was waiting
for her. In a voice that might have been contrite, but seemed in
fact frightened, he said, "That's a nice baby."

Juliet said, "Thank you."

She thought that now they might properly say good-bye, but
something was holding him. He continued to look at her, he did
not move away. He put his hand out as if to catch hold of her
shoulder, then dropped it.

"Do you know if you have——," he said, then shook his head
slightly. The *have* had come out sounding like *hab*.

"Jooze," he said, and slapped his hand against his throat. He
waved in the direction of the kitchen.

Juliet's first thought was that he must be drunk. His head was
wagging slightly back and forth, his eyes seemed to be filmed
over. Had he come here drunk, had he brought something in
his pocket? Then she remembered. A girl, a pupil at the school
where she had once taught for half a year. This girl, a diabetic, would suffer a kind of seizure, become thick-tongued,
distraught, staggering, if she had gone too long without food.

Shifting Penelope to her hip, she took hold of his arm and
steadied him along towards the kitchen. Juice. That was what
they had given the girl, that was what he was talking about.

"Just a minute, just a minute, you'll be all right," she said. He held himself upright, hands pressed down on the counter, head lowered.

There was no orange juice—she remembered giving Penelope the last of it that morning, thinking she must get more. But there was a bottle of grape soda, which Sam and Irene liked to drink when they came in from work in the garden.

"Here," she said. Managing with one hand, as she was used to doing, she poured out a glassful. "Here." And as he drank she said, "I'm sorry there's no juice. But it's the sugar, isn't it? You have to get some sugar?"

He drank it down, he said, "Yeah. Sugar. Thanks." Already his voice was clearing. She remembered this too, about the girl at the school—how quick and apparently miraculous the recovery. But before he was quite recovered, or quite himself, while he was still holding his head at a slant, he met her eyes. Not on purpose, it seemed, just by chance. The look in his eyes was not grateful, or forgiving—it was not really personal, it was just the raw look of an astounded animal, hanging on to whatever it could find.

And within a few seconds the eyes, the face, became the face of the man, the minister, who set down his glass and without another word fled out of the house.

Sara was either asleep or pretending to be, when Juliet went to pick up the tea tray. Her sleeping state, her dozing state, and her waking state had now such delicate and shifting boundaries that it was hard to identify them. At any rate, she spoke, she said in little more than a whisper, "Juliet?"

Juliet paused in the doorway.

"You must think Don is—rather a simpleton," Sara said. "But he isn't well. He's a diabetic. It's serious."

Juliet said, "Yes."

"He needs his faith."

"Foxhole argument," said Juliet, but quietly, and perhaps Sara did not hear, for she went on talking.

"My faith isn't so simple," said Sara, her voice all shaky (and seeming to Juliet, at this moment, strategically pathetic). "I can't describe it. But it's—all I can say—it's *something*. It's a— wonderful—*something*. When it gets really bad for me—when it gets so bad I—you know what I think then? I think, all right. I think— Soon. *Soon I'll see Juliet*."

> *Dreaded (Dearest) Eric,*
>
> *Where to begin? I am fine and Penelope is fine. Considering. She walks confidently now around Sara's bed but is still leery of striking out with no support. The summer heat is amazing, compared with the west coast. Even when it rains. It's a good thing it does rain because Sam is going full-tilt at the market garden business. The other day I rode around with him in the ancient vehicle delivering fresh raspberries and raspberry jam (made by a sort of junior Ilse Koch person who inhabits our kitchen) and newly dug first potatoes of the season. He is quite gungho. Sara stays in bed and dozes or looks at outdated fashion magazines. A minister came to visit her and he and I got into a big stupid row about the existence of God or some such hot topic. The visit is going okay though . . .*

This was a letter that Juliet found years later Eric must have saved it by accident—it had no particular importance in their lives.

. . .

She had gone back to the house of her childhood once more, for Sara's funeral, some months after that letter was written. Irene was no longer around, and Juliet had no memory of asking or being told where she was. Most probably she had married. As Sam did again, in a couple of years. He married a fellow teacher, a good-natured, handsome, competent woman. They lived in her house—Sam tore down the house where he and Sara had lived, and extended the garden. When his wife retired, they bought a trailer and began to go on long winter trips. They visited Juliet twice at Whale Bay. Eric took them out in his boat. He and Sam got along well. As Sam said, like a house afire.

When she read the letter, Juliet winced, as anybody does on discovering the preserved and disconcerting voice of some past fabricated self. She wondered at the sprightly cover-up, contrasting with the pain of her memories. Then she thought that some shift must have taken place, at that time, which she had not remembered. Some shift concerning where home was. Not at Whale Bay with Eric but back where it had been before, all her life before.

Because it's what happens at home that you try to protect, as best you can, for as long as you can.

But she had not protected Sara. When Sara had said, *soon I'll see Juliet,* Juliet had found no reply. Could it not have been managed? Why should it have been so difficult? Just to say *Yes.* To Sara it would have meant so much—to herself, surely, so little. But she had turned away, she had carried the tray to the kitchen, and there she washed and dried the cups and also the glass that had held grape soda. She had put everything away.

SILENCE

———◆———

On the short ferry ride from Buckley Bay to Denman Island, Juliet got out of her car and stood at the front of the boat, in the summer breeze. A woman standing there recognized her, and they began to talk. It is not unusual for people to take a second look at Juliet and wonder where they've seen her before, and, sometimes, to remember. She appears regularly on the Provincial Television channel, interviewing people who are leading singular or notable lives, and doftly directing panel discussions, on a program called *Issues of the Day*. Her hair is cut short now, as short as possible, and has taken on a very dark auburn color, matching the frames of her glasses. She often wears black pants—as she does today—and an ivory silk shirt, and sometimes a black jacket. She is what her mother would have called a striking-looking woman.

"Forgive me. People must be always bothering you."

"It's okay," Juliet says. "Except when I've just been to the dentist or something."

The woman is about Juliet's age. Long black hair streaked with gray, no makeup, long denim skirt. She lives on Denman, so Juliet asks her what she knows about the Spiritual Balance Centre.

"Because my daughter is there," Juliet says. "She's been on a retreat there or taking a course, I don't know what they call it. For six months. This is the first time I've got to see her, in six months."

"There are a couple of places like that," the woman says. "They sort of come and go. I don't mean there's anything suspect about them. Just that they're generally off in the woods, you know, and don't have much to do with the community. Well, what would be the point of a retreat if they did?"

She says that Juliet must be looking forward to seeing her daughter again, and Juliet says yes, very much.

"I'm spoiled," she says. "She's twenty years old, my daughter—she'll be twenty-one this month, actually—and we haven't been apart much."

The woman says that she has a son of twenty and a daughter of eighteen and another of fifteen, and there are days when she'd *pay* them to go on a retreat, singly or all together.

Juliet laughs. "Well. I've only the one. Of course, I won't guarantee that I won't be all for shipping her back, given a few weeks."

This is the kind of fond but exasperated mother-talk she finds it easy to slip into (Juliet is an expert at reassuring responses), but the truth is that Penelope has scarcely ever given her cause for complaint, and if she wanted to be totally honest, at this point she would say that one day without some contact with her daughter is hard to bear, let alone six months. Penelope has worked at Banff, as a summer chambermaid, and she has gone on bus trips to Mexico, a hitchhiking trip to Newfoundland. But she has always lived with Juliet, and there has never been a six-month break.

She gives me delight, Juliet could have said. *Not that she is one of those song-and-dance purveyors of sunshine and cheer and looking-on-the-bright-side. I hope I've brought her up better than that. She has grace and compassion and she is as wise as if she'd been on this earth for eighty years. Her nature is reflective, not all over the map like mine. Somewhat reticent, like her father's. She is also angelically pretty, she's like my mother, blond like my mother but not so frail. Strong and noble. Molded, I should say, like a caryatid. And contrary to popular notions I am not even faintly jealous. All this time without her—and with no word from her, because Spiritual Balance does not allow letters or phone calls—all this time I've been in a sort of desert, and when her message came I was like an old patch of cracked earth getting a full drink of rain.*

Hope to see you Sunday afternoon. It's time.

Time to go home, was what Juliet hoped this meant, but of course she would leave that up to Penelope.

Penelope had drawn a rudimentary map, and Juliet shortly found herself parked in front of an old church—that is, a church building seventy-five or eighty years old, covered with stucco, not as old or anything like as impressive as churches usually were in the part of Canada where Juliet had grown up. Behind it was a more recent building, with a slanting roof and windows all across its front, also a simple stage and some seating benches and what looked like a volleyball court with a sagging net. Everything was shabby, and the once-cleared patch of land was being reclaimed by juniper and poplars.

A couple of people—she could not tell whether men or women—were doing some carpentry work on the stage, and others sat on the benches in separate small groups. All wore ordinary clothes, not yellow robes or anything of that sort. For a few minutes no notice was taken of Juliet's car. Then one of the people on the benches rose and walked unhurriedly towards her. A short, middle-aged man wearing glasses.

She got out of the car and greeted him and asked for Penelope. He did not speak—perhaps there was a rule of silence—but nodded and turned away and went into the church. From which there shortly appeared, not Penelope, but a heavy, slow-moving woman with white hair, wearing jeans and a baggy sweater.

"What an honor to meet you," she said. "Do come inside. I've asked Donny to make us some tea."

She had a broad fresh face, a smile both roguish and tender, and what Juliet supposed must be called twinkling eyes. "My name is Joan," she said. Juliet had been expecting an assumed name like Serenity, or something with an Eastern flavor, nothing so plain and familiar as Joan. Later, of course, she thought of Pope Joan.

"I've got the right place, have I? I'm a stranger on Denman," she said disarmingly. "You know I've come to see Penelope?"

"Of course. Penelope." Joan prolonged the name, with a certain tone of celebration.

The inside of the church was darkened with purple cloth hung over the high windows. The pews and other church furnishings had been removed, and plain white curtains had been strung up to form private cubicles, as in a hospital ward. The cubicle into which Juliet was directed had, however, no bed, just a small table and a couple of plastic chairs, and some open shelves piled untidily with loose papers.

"I'm afraid we're still in the process of getting things fixed up in here," Joan said. "Juliet. May I call you Juliet?"

"Yes, of course."

"I'm not used to talking to a celebrity." Joan held her hands together in a prayer pose beneath her chin. "I don't know whether to be informal or not."

"I'm not much of a celebrity."

"Oh, you are. Now don't say things like that. And I'll just get it off my chest right away, how I admire you for the work you do. It's a beam in the darkness. The only television worth watching."

"Thank you," said Juliet. "I had a note from Penelope—"

"I know. But I'm sorry to have to tell you, Juliet, I'm very sorry and I don't want you to be too disappointed—Penelope is not here."

The woman says those words—*Penelope is not here*—as lightly as possible. You would think that Penelope's absence could be turned into a matter for amused contemplation, even for their mutual delight.

Juliet has to take a deep breath. For a moment she cannot speak. Dread pours through her. Foreknowledge. Then she pulls herself back to reasonable consideration of this fact. She fishes around in her bag.

"She said she hoped—"

"I know. I know," says Joan. "She did intend to be here, but the fact was, she could not—"

"Where is she? Where did she go?"

"I cannot tell you that."

"You mean you can't or you won't?"

"I can't. I don't know. But I can tell you one thing that may put your mind at rest. Wherever she has gone, whatever she has decided, it will be the right thing for her. It will be the *right* thing for her spirituality and her growth."

Juliet decides to let this pass. She gags on the word *spiritu-ality*, which seems to take in—as she often says—everything from prayer wheels to High Mass. She never expected that Penelope, with her intelligence, would be mixed up in anything like this.

"I just thought I should know," she says, "in case she wanted me to send on any of her things."

"Her possessions?" Joan seems unable to suppress a wide smile, though she modifies it at once with an expression of tenderness. "Penelope is not very concerned right now about her *possessions.*"

Sometimes Juliet has felt, in the middle of an interview, that the person she faces has reserves of hostility that were not apparent before the cameras started rolling. A person whom Juliet has underestimated, whom she has thought rather stupid, may have strength of that sort. Playful but deadly hostility. The thing then is never to show that you are taken aback, never to display any hint of hostility in return.

"What I mean by growth is our inward growth, of course," Joan says.

"I understand," says Juliet, looking her in the eye.

"Penelope has had such a wonderful opportunity in her life to meet interesting people—goodness, she hasn't needed to meet interesting people, she's *grown up* with an interesting person, you're her *mother*—but you know, sometimes there's a dimension that is missing, grown-up children feel that they've *missed out* on something—"

"Oh yes," says Juliet. "I know that grown-up children can have all sorts of complaints."

Joan has decided to come down hard.

"The spiritual dimension—I have to say this—was it not altogether lacking in Penelope's life? I take it she did not grow up in a faith-based home."

"Religion was not a banned subject. We could talk about it."

"But perhaps it was the way you talked about it. Your intellectual way? If you know what I mean. You are so clever," she adds, kindly.

"So you say."

Juliet is aware that any control of the interview, and of herself, is faltering, and may be lost.

"Not so *I* say, Juliet. So *Penelope* says. Penelope is a dear fine girl, but she has come to us here in great hunger. Hunger for the things that were not available to her in her home. There you were, with your wonderful busy successful life—but Juliet, I must tell you that your daughter has known loneliness. She has known unhappiness."

"Don't most people feel that, one time or another? Loneliness and unhappiness?"

"It's not for me to say. Oh, Juliet. You are a woman of marvellous insights. I've often watched you on television and I've thought, how does she get right to the heart of things like that, and all the time being so nice and polite to people? I never thought I'd be sitting talking to you face-to-face. And what's more, that I'd be in a position to *help* you—"

"I think that maybe you're mistaken about that."

"You feel hurt. It's natural that you should feel hurt."

"It's also my own business."

"Ah well. Perhaps she'll get in touch with you. After all."

Penelope did get in touch with Juliet, a couple of weeks later. A birthday card arrived on her own—Penelope's—birthday, the 19th of June. Her twenty-first birthday. It was the sort of card you send to an acquaintance whose tastes you cannot guess. Not a crude jokey card or a truly witty card or a sentimental card. On the front of it was a small bouquet of pansies tied by a thin purple ribbon whose tail spelled out the words *Happy Birthday*. These words were repeated inside, with the words *Wishing you a very* added in gold letters above them.

And there was no signature. Juliet thought at first that someone had sent this card to Penelope, and forgotten to sign it, and that she, Juliet, had opened it by mistake. Someone who had Penelope's name and the date of her birth on file. Her dentist, maybe, or her driving teacher. But when she checked the writing on the envelope she saw that there had been no mistake— there was her own name, indeed, written in Penelope's own handwriting.

Postmarks gave you no clue anymore. They all said *Canada Post*. Juliet had some idea that there were ways of telling at least which province a letter came from, but for that you would have to consult the Post Office, go there with the letter and very likely be called upon to prove your case, your right to the information. And somebody would be sure to recognize her.

She went to see her old friend Christa, who had lived in Whale Bay when she herself lived there, even before Penelope was born. Christa was in Kitsilano, in an assisted-living facility. She had multiple sclerosis. Her room was on the ground floor, with a small private patio, and Juliet sat with her there, looking out at a sunny bit of lawn, and the wisteria all in bloom along the fence that concealed the garbage bins.

Juliet told Christa the whole story of the trip to Denman Island. She had told nobody else, and had hoped perhaps not to have to tell anybody. Every day when she was on her way home from work she had wondered if perhaps Penelope would be waiting in the apartment. Or at least that there would be a letter. And then there had been—that unkind card—and she had torn it open with her hands shaking.

"It means something," Christa said. "It lets you know she's okay. Something will follow. It will. Be patient."

Juliet talked bitterly for a while about Mother Shipton. That was what she finally decided to call her, having toyed with and become dissatisfied with Pope Joan. What bloody chicanery, she said. What creepiness, nastiness, behind the second-rate, sweetly religious facade. It was impossible to imagine Penelope's having been taken in by her.

Christa suggested that perhaps Penelope had visited the place because she had considered writing something about it. Some sort of investigative journalism. Fieldwork. The personal angle—the long-winded personal stuff that was so popular nowadays.

Investigating for six months? said Juliet. Penelope could have figured out Mother Shipton in ten minutes.

"It's weird," admitted Christa.

"You don't know more than you're letting on, do you?" said Juliet. "I hate to even ask that. I feel so at sea. I feel stupid. That woman intended me to feel stupid, of course. Like the character who blurts out something in a play and everybody turns away because they all know something she doesn't know—"

"They don't do that kind of play anymore," Christa said. "Now nobody knows anything. No—Penelope didn't take me into her confidence any more than she did you. Why should she? She'd know I'd end up telling you."

Juliet was quiet for a moment, then she muttered sulkily, "There have been things you didn't tell me."

"Oh, for God's sake," said Christa, but without any animosity. "Not that again."

"Not that again," Juliet agreed. "I'm in a lousy mood, that's all."

"Just hold on. One of the trials of parenthood. She hasn't

given you many, after all. In a year this will all be ancient history."

Juliet didn't tell her that in the end she had not been able to walk away with dignity. She had turned and cried out beseechingly, furiously.

"What did she tell you?"

And Mother Shipton was standing there watching her, as if she had expected this. A fat pitying smile had stretched her closed lips as she shook her head.

During the next year Juliet would get phone calls, now and then, from people who had been friendly with Penelope. Her reply to their inquiries was always the same. Penelope had decided to take a year off. She was travelling. Her travelling agenda was by no means fixed, and Juliet had no way of contacting her, nor any address she could supply.

She did not hear from anybody who had been a close friend. This might mean that people who had been close to Penelope knew quite well where she was. Or it might be that they too were off on trips to foreign countries, had found jobs in other provinces, were embarked on new lives, too crowded or chancy at present to allow them to wonder about old friends.

(Old friends, at that stage in life, meaning somebody you had not seen for half a year.)

Whenever she came in, the first thing Juliet did was to look for the light flashing on her answering machine—the very thing she used to avoid, thinking there would be someone pestering her about her public utterances. She tried various silly tricks, to do with how many steps she took to the phone, how she picked it up, how she breathed. *Let it be her.*

Nothing worked. After a while the world seemed emptied

of the people Penelope had known, the boyfriends she had dropped and the ones who had dropped her, the girls she had gossiped with and probably confided in. She had gone to a private girls' boarding school—Torrance House—rather than to a public high school, and this meant that most of her longtime friends—even those who were still her friends at college—had come from places out of town. Some from Alaska or Prince George or Peru.

There was no message at Christmas. But in June, another card, very much in the style of the first, not a word written inside. Juliet had a drink of wine before she opened it, then threw it away at once. She had spurts of weeping, once in a while of uncontrollable shaking, but she came out of these in quick fits of fury, walking around the house and slapping one fist into her palm. The fury was directed at Mother Shipton, but the image of that woman had faded, and finally Juliet had to recognize that she was really only a convenience.

All pictures of Penelope were banished to her bedroom, with sheaves of drawings and crayonings she had done before they left Whale Bay, her books, and the European one-cup coffee-maker with the plunger that she had bought as a present for Juliet with the first money she had made in her summer job at McDonald's. Also such whimsical gifts for the apartment as a tiny plastic fan to stick on the refrigerator, a wind-up toy tractor, a curtain of glass beads to hang in the bathroom window. The door of that bedroom was shut and in time could be passed without disturbance.

Juliet gave a great deal of thought to getting out of this apartment, giving herself the benefit of new surroundings. But she said to Christa that she could not do that, because that was the address Penelope had, and mail could be forwarded for only three months, so there would be no place then where her daughter could find her.

"She could always get to you at work," said Christa.

"Who knows how long I'll be there?" Juliet said. "She's probably in some commune where they're not allowed to communicate. With some guru who sleeps with all the women and sends them out to beg on the streets. If I'd sent her to Sunday school and taught her to say her prayers this probably wouldn't have happened. I should have. I should have. It would have been like an inoculation. I neglected her *spirituality*. Mother Shipton said so."

When Penelope was barely thirteen years old, she had gone away on a camping trip to the Kootenay Mountains of British Columbia, with a friend from Torrance House, and the friend's family. Juliet was in favor of this. Penelope had been at Torrance House for only one year (accepted on favorable financial terms because of her mother's once having taught there), and it pleased Juliet that she had already made so firm a friend and been accepted readily by the friend's family. Also that she was going camping—something that regular children did and that Juliet, as a child, had never had the chance to do. Not that she would have wanted to, being already buried in books—but she welcomed signs that Penelope was turning out to be a more normal sort of girl than she herself had been.

Eric was apprehensive about the whole idea. He thought Penelope was too young. He didn't like her going on a holiday with people he knew so little about. And now that she went to boarding school they saw too little of her as it was—so why should that time be shortened?

Juliet had another reason—she simply wanted Penelope out of the way for the first couple of weeks of the summer holidays, because the air was not clear between herself and Eric. She wanted things resolved, and they were not resolved. She did not want to have to pretend that all was well, for the sake of the child.

Eric, on the other hand, would have liked nothing better than to see their trouble smoothed over, hidden out of the way. To Eric's way of thinking, civility would restore good feeling, the semblance of love would be enough to get by on until love itself might be rediscovered. And if there was never anything more than a semblance—well, that would have to do. Eric could manage with that.

Indeed he could, thought Juliet, despondently.

Having Penelope at home, a reason for them to behave well—for Juliet to behave well, since she was the one, in his opinion, who stirred up all the rancor—that would suit Eric very well.

So Juliet told him, and created a new source of bitterness and blame, because he missed Penelope badly.

The reason for their quarrel was an old and ordinary one. In the spring, through some trivial disclosure—and the frankness or possibly the malice of their longtime neighbor Ailo, who had a certain loyalty to Eric's dead wife and some reservations about Juliet—Juliet had discovered that Eric had slept with Christa. Christa had been for a long time her close friend, but she had been, before that, Eric's girlfriend, his *mistress* (though nobody said that anymore). He had given her up when he asked Juliet to live with him. She had known all about Christa then and she could not reasonably object to what had happened in the time before she and Eric were together. She did not. What she did object to—what she claimed had broken her heart—had happened after that. (But still a long time ago, said Eric.) It had happened when Penelope was a year old, and Juliet had taken her back to Ontario. When Juliet had gone home to visit her parents. To visit—as she always pointed out now—to visit her dying mother. When she was away, and loving and missing Eric with every shred of her being (she now believed this), Eric had simply returned to his old habits.

At first he confessed to once (drunk), but with further prodding, and some drinking in the here-and-now, he said that possibly it had been more often.

Possibly? He could not remember? So many times he could not remember?

He could remember.

Christa came to see Juliet, to assure her that it had been nothing serious. (This was Eric's refrain, as well.) Juliet told her to go away and never come back. Christa decided that now would be a good time to go to see her brother in California.

Juliet's outrage at Christa was actually something of a formality. She did understand that a few rolls in the hay with an old girlfriend (Eric's disastrous description, his ill-judged attempt to minimize things) were nowhere near as threatening as a hot embrace with some woman newly met. Also, her outrage at Eric was so fierce and irrepressible as to leave little room for blame of anybody else.

Her contentions were that he did not love her, had never loved her, had mocked her, with Christa, behind her back. He had made her a laughingstock in front of people like Ailo (who had always hated her). That he had treated her with contempt, he regarded the love she felt (or had felt) for him with contempt, he had lived a lie with her. Sex meant nothing to him, or at any rate it did not mean what it meant (had meant) to her, he would have it off with whoever was handy.

Only the last of these contentions had the least germ of truth in it, and in her quieter states she knew that. But even that little truth was enough to pull everything down around her. It shouldn't do that, but it did. And Eric was not able—in all honesty he was not able—to see why that should be so. He was not surprised that she should object, make a fuss, even weep (though a woman like Christa would never have done that), but that she should really be damaged, that she should consider herself bereft of all that had sustained her—and for something that had happened *twelve years ago*—this he could not understand.

Sometimes he believed that she was shamming, making the most of it, and at other times he was full of real grief, that he had made her suffer. Their grief aroused them, and they made love magnificently. And each time he thought that would be the end of it, their miseries were over. Each time he was mistaken.

In bed, Juliet laughed and told him about Pepys and Mrs. Pepys, inflamed with passion under similar circumstances. (Since more or less giving up on her classical studies, she was reading widely, and nowadays everything she read seemed to have to do with adultery.) Never so often and never so hot, Pepys had said, though he recorded as well that his wife had also thought of murdering him in his sleep. Juliet laughed about this, but half an hour later, when he came to say good-bye before going out in the boat to check his prawn traps, she showed a stony face and gave him a kiss of resignation, as if he'd been going to meet a woman out in the middle of the bay and under a rainy sky.

There was more than rain. The water was hardly choppy when Eric went out, but later in the afternoon a wind came up suddenly, from the southeast, and tore up the waters of Desolation Sound and Malaspina Strait. It continued almost till dark—which did not really close down until around eleven o'clock in this last week of June. By then a sailboat from Campbell River was missing, with three adults and two children aboard. Also two fish boats—one with two men aboard and the other with only one man—Eric.

The next morning was calm and sunny—the mountains, the waters, the shores, all sleek and sparkling.

It was possible, of course, that none of these people were lost, that they had found shelter and spent the night in any of the multitude of little bays. That was more likely to be true of the fishermen than of the family in the sailboat, who were not local people but vacationers from Seattle. Boats went out at once, that morning, to search the mainland and island shores and the water.

The drowned children were found first, in their life jackets, and by the end of the day the bodies of their parents were located as well. A grandfather who had accompanied them was not found until the day after. The bodies of the men who had been fishing together never showed up, though the remnants of their boat washed up near Refuge Cove.

Eric's body was recovered on the third day. Juliet was not allowed to see it. Something had got at him, it was said (meaning some animal), after the body was washed ashore.

It was perhaps because of this—because there was no question of viewing the body and no need for an undertaker—that the idea caught hold amongst Eric's old friends and fellow fishermen of burning Eric on the beach. Juliet did not object to this. A death certificate had to be made out, so the doctor who came to Whale Bay once a week was telephoned at his office in Powell River, and he gave Ailo, who was his weekly assistant and a registered nurse, the authority to do this.

There was plenty of driftwood around, plenty of the sea-salted bark which makes a superior fire. In a couple of hours all was ready. News had spread—somehow, even at such short notice, women began arriving with food. It was Ailo who took charge—her Scandinavian blood, her upright carriage and flowing white hair, seeming to fit her naturally for the role of Widow of the Sea. Children ran about on the logs, and were shooed away from the growing pyre, the shrouded, surprisingly meager bundle that was Eric. A coffee urn was supplied to this half-pagan ceremony by the women from one of the churches, and cartons of beer, bottles of drink of all sorts, were left discreetly, for the time being, in the trunks of cars and cabs of trucks.

The question arose of who would speak, and who would light the pyre. They asked Juliet, would she do it? And Juliet— brittle and busy, handing out mugs of coffee—said that they had it wrong, as the widow she was supposed to throw herself into the flames. She actually laughed as she said this, and those who had asked her backed off, afraid that she was getting hysterical. The man who had partnered Eric most often in the boat agreed to do the lighting, but said he was no speaker. It occurred to some that he would not have been a good choice anyway, since his wife was an Evangelical Anglican, and he might have felt obliged to say things which would have distressed Eric if he had been able to hear them. Then Ailo's husband offered—he was a little man disfigured by a fire on a boat, years ago, a grumbling socialist and atheist, and in his talk he rather lost track of Eric, except to claim him as a Brother in the Battle. He went on at surprising length, and this was ascribed, afterwards, to the suppressed life he led under the rule of Ailo. There might have been some restlessness in the crowd before his recital of grievances got stopped, some feeling that the event was turning out to be not so splendid, or solemn, or heartrending, as might have been expected. But when the fire began to burn this feeling vanished, and there was great concentration, even, or especially, among the children, until the moment when one of the men cried, "Get the kids out of here." This was when the flames had reached the body, bringing the realization, coming rather late, that consumption of fat, of heart and kidneys and liver, might produce explosive or sizzling noises disconcerting to hear. So a good many of the children were hauled away by their mothers—some willingly, some to their own dismay. So the final act of the fire became a mostly male ceremony, and slightly scandalous, even if not, in this case, illegal.

Juliet stayed, wide-eyed, rocking on her haunches, face pressed against the heat. She was not quite there. She thought of whoever it was—Trelawny?—snatching Shelley's heart out of the flames. The heart, with its long history of significance. Strange to think how even at that time, not so long ago, one fleshly organ should be thought so precious, the site of courage and love. It was just flesh, burning. Nothing connected with Eric.

Penelope knew nothing of what was going on. There was a short item in the Vancouver paper—not about the burning on the beach, of course, just about the drowning—but no newspapers or radio reports reached her, deep in the Kootenay Mountains. When she got back to Vancouver she phoned home, from her friend Heather's house. Christa answered—she had got back too late for the ceremony, but was staying with Juliet, and helping as she could. Christa said that Juliet was not there—it was a lie—and asked to speak to Heather's mother. She explained what had happened, and said that she was driving Juliet to Vancouver, they would leave at once, and Juliet would tell Penelope herself when they got there.

Christa dropped Juliet at the house where Penelope was, and Juliet went inside alone. Heather's mother left her in the sunroom, where Penelope was waiting. Penelope received the news with an expression of fright, then—when Juliet rather formally put her arms around her—of something like embarrassment. Perhaps in Heather's house, in the white and green and orange sunroom, with Heather's brothers shooting baskets in the backyard, news so dire could hardly penetrate. The burning was not mentioned—in this house and neighborhood it would surely have seemed uncivilized, grotesque. In this house, also, Juliet's manner was sprightly beyond anything intended—her behavior close to that of *a good sport*.

Heather's mother entered after a tiny knock—with glasses of iced tea. Penelope gulped hers down and went to join Heather, who had been lurking in the hall.

Heather's mother then had a talk with Juliet. She apologized for intruding with practical matters but said that time was short. She and Heather's father were driving east in a few days' time to see relatives. They would be gone for a month, and had planned to take Heather with them. (The boys were going to camp.) But now Heather had decided she did not want to go, she had begged to stay here in the house, with Penelope. A fourteen-year-old and a thirteen-year-old could not really be left alone, and it had occurred to her that Juliet might like some time away, a respite, after what she had been through. After her loss and tragedy.

So Juliet shortly found herself living in a different world, in a large spotless house brightly and thoughtfully decorated, with what are called conveniences—but to her were luxuries—on every hand. This on a curving street lined with similar houses, behind trimmed bushes and showy flower beds. Even the weather, for that month, was flawless—warm, breezy, bright. Heather and Penelope went swimming, played badminton in the backyard, went to the movies, baked cookies, gorged, dieted, worked on their tans, filled the house with music whose lyrics seemed to Juliet sappy and irritating, sometimes invited girlfriends over, did not exactly invite boys but held long, taunting, aimless conversations with some who passed the house or had collected next door. By chance, Juliet heard Penelope say to one of the visiting girls, "Well, I hardly knew him, really."

She was speaking about her father.

How strange.

She had never been afraid to go out in the boat, as Juliet was, when there was a chop on the water. She had pestered him to be taken and was often successful. When following after Eric, in her businesslike orange life jacket, carrying what gear she could manage, she always wore an expression of particular seriousness and dedication. She took note of the setting of the traps and became skilful, quick, and ruthless at the deheading and bagging of the catch. At a certain stage of her childhood—say from eight to eleven—she had always said that she was going to go out fishing when she grew up, and Eric had told her there were girls doing that nowadays. Juliet had thought it was possible, since Penelope was bright but not bookish, and exuberantly physical, and brave. But Eric, out of Penelope's hearing, said that he hoped the idea would wear off, he wouldn't wish the life on anybody. He always spoke this way, about the hardship and uncertainty of the work he had chosen, but took pride, so Juliet thought, in those very things.

And now he was dismissed. By Penelope, who had recently painted her toenails purple and was sporting a false tattoo on her midriff. He who had filled her life. She dismissed him.

But Juliet felt as if she was doing the same. Of course, she was busy looking for a job and a place to live. She had already put the house in Whale Bay up for sale—she could not imagine remaining there. She had sold the truck and given away Eric's tools, and such traps as had been recovered, and the dinghy. Eric's grown son from Saskatchewan had come and taken the dog.

She had applied for a job in the reference department of the college library, and a job in the public library, and she had a feeling she would get one or the other. She looked at apartments in the Kitsilano or Dunbar or Point Grey areas. The cleanness, tidiness, and manageability of city life kept surprising her. This was how people lived where the man's work did not take place out of doors, and where various operations connected with it did not end up indoors. And where the weather might be a factor in your mood but never in your life, where such dire matters as the changing habits and availability of prawns and salmon were merely interesting, or not remarked upon at all. The life she had been leading at Whale Bay, such a short time ago, seemed haphazard, cluttered, exhausting, by comparison. And she herself was cleansed of the moods of the last months—she was brisk and competent, and better-looking.

Eric should see her now.

She thought about Eric in this way all the time. It was not that she failed to realize that Eric was dead—that did not happen for a moment. But nevertheless she kept constantly referring to him, in her mind, as if he was still the person to whom her existence mattered more than it could to anyone else. As if he was still the person in whose eyes she hoped to shine. Also the person to whom she presented arguments, information, surprises. This was such a habit with her, and took place so automatically, that the fact of his death did not seem to interfere with it.

Nor was their last quarrel entirely resolved. She held him to account, still, for his betrayal. When she flaunted herself a little now, it was against that.

The storm, the recovery of the body, the burning on the beach—that was all like a pageant she had been compelled to watch and compelled to believe in, which still had nothing to do with Eric and herself.

.   .   .

She got the job in the reference library, she found a two-bedroom apartment that she could just afford, Penelope went back to Torrance House as a day student. Their affairs at Whale Bay were wound up, their life there finished. Even Christa was moving out, coming to Vancouver in the spring.

On a day before that, a day in February, Juliet stood in the shelter at the campus bus stop when her afternoon's work was over. The day's rain had stopped, there was a band of clear sky in the west, red where the sun had gone down, out over the Strait of Georgia. This sign of the lengthening days, the promise of the change of season, had an effect on her that was unexpected and crushing.

She realized that Eric was dead.

As if all this time, while she was in Vancouver, he had been waiting somewhere, waiting to see if she would resume her life with him. As if being with him was an option that had stayed open. Her life since she came here had still been lived against a backdrop of Eric, without her ever quite understanding that Eric did not exist. Nothing of him existed. The memory of him in the daily and ordinary world was in retreat.

So this is grief. She feels as if a sack of cement has been poured into her and quickly hardened. She can barely move. Getting onto the bus, getting off the bus, walking half a block to her building (why is she living here?), is like climbing a cliff. And now she must hide this from Penelope.

At the supper table she began to shake, but could not loosen her fingers to drop the knife and fork. Penelope came around the table and pried her hands open. She said, "It's Dad, isn't it?"

Juliet afterwards told a few people—such as Christa—that these seemed the most utterly absolving, the most tender words, that anybody had ever said to her.

Penelope ran her cool hands up and down the insides of Juliet's arms. She phoned the library the next day to say that her mother was sick, and she took care of her for a couple of days, staying home from school until Juliet recovered. Or until, at least, the worst was over.

During those days Juliet told Penelope everything. Christa, the fight, the burning on the beach (which she had so far managed, almost miraculously, to conceal from her). Everything.

"I shouldn't burden you with all this."

Penelope said, "Yeah, well, maybe not." But added staunchly, "I forgive you. I guess I'm not a baby."

Juliet went back into the world. The sort of fit she had had in the bus stop recurred, but never so powerfully.

Through her research work in the library, she met some people from the Provincial Television channel, and took a job they offered. She had worked there for about a year when she began to do interviews. All the indiscriminate reading she'd done for years (and that Ailo had so disapproved of, in the days at Whale Bay), all the bits and pieces of information she'd picked up, her random appetite and quick assimilation, were now to come in handy. And she cultivated a self-deprecating, faintly teasing manner that usually seemed to go over well. On camera, few things fazed her. Though in fact she would go home and march back and forth, letting out whimpers or curses as she recalled some perceived glitch or fluster or, worse still, a mispronunciation.

After five years the birthday cards stopped coming.

"It doesn't mean anything," Christa said. "All they were for was to tell you she's alive somewhere. Now she figures you've got the message. She trusts you not to send some tracker after her. That's all."

"Did I put too much on her?"

"Oh, Jul."

"I don't mean just with Eric dying. Other men, later. I let her see too much misery. My stupid misery."

For Juliet had had two affairs during the years that Penelope was between fourteen and twenty-one, and during both of these she had managed to fall hectically in love, though she was ashamed afterwards. One of the men was much older than she, and solidly married. The other was a good deal younger, and was alarmed by her ready emotions. Later she wondered at these herself. She really had cared nothing for him, she said.

"I wouldn't think you did," said Christa, who was tired. "I don't know."

"Oh Christ. I was such a fool. I don't get like that about men anymore. Do I?"

Christa did not mention that this might be because of a lack of candidates.

"No, Jul. No."

"Actually I didn't do anything so terrible," Juliet said then, brightening up. "Why do I keep lamenting that it's my fault? She's a conundrum, that's all. I need to face that.

"A conundrum and a cold fish," she said, in a parody of resolution.

"No," said Christa.

"No," said Juliet. "No—that's not true."

After the second June had passed without any word, Juliet decided to move. For the first five years, she told Christa, she had waited for June, wondering what might come. The way things were now, she had to wonder every day. And be disappointed every day.

She moved to a high-rise building in the West End. She meant to throw away the contents of Penelope's room, but in the end she stuffed it all into garbage bags and carried it with her. She had only one bedroom now but there was storage space in the basement.

She took up jogging in Stanley Park. Now she seldom mentioned Penelope, even to Christa. She had a boyfriend—that was what you called them now—who had never heard anything about her daughter.

Christa grew thinner and moodier. Quite suddenly, one January, she died.

You don't go on forever, appearing on television. However agreeable the viewers have found your face, there comes a time when they'd prefer somebody different. Juliet was offered other jobs—researching, writing voice-over for nature shows—but she refused them cheerfully, describing herself as in need of a total change. She went back to Classical Studies—an even smaller department than it used to be—she meant to resume writing her thesis for her Ph.D. She moved out of the high-rise apartment and into a bachelor flat, to save money.

Her boyfriend had got a teaching job in China.

Her flat was in the basement of a house, but the sliding doors at the back opened out at ground level. And there she had a little brick-paved patio, a trellis with sweet peas and clematis, herbs and flowers in pots. For the first time in her life, and in a very small way, she was a gardener, as her father had been.

Sometimes people said to her—in stores, or on the campus bus—"Excuse me, but your face is so familiar," or, "Aren't you the lady that used to be on television?" But after a year or so this passed. She spent a lot of time sitting and reading, drinking coffee at sidewalk tables, and nobody noticed her. She let her hair grow out. During the years that it had been dyed red it had lost the vigor of its natural brown—it was a silvery brown now, fine and wavy. She was reminded of her mother, Sara. Sara's soft, fair, flyaway hair, going gray and then white.

She did not have room to have people to dinner anymore, and

she had lost interest in recipes. She ate meals that were nourish-
ing enough, but monotonous. Without exactly meaning to, she
lost contact with most of her friends.

It was no wonder. She lived now a life as different as possible
from the life of the public, vivacious, concerned, endlessly well-
informed woman that she had been. She lived amongst books,
reading through most of her waking hours and being compelled
to deepen, to alter, whatever premise she had started with. She
often missed the world news for a week at a time.

She had given up on her thesis and become interested in some
writers referred to as the Greek novelists, whose work came
rather late in the history of Greek literature (starting in the first
century B.C.E., as she had now learned to call it, and continuing
into the early Middle Ages). Aristeides, Longus, Heliodorus,
Achilles Tatius. Much of their work is lost or fragmentary and is
also reported to be indecent. But there is a romance written by
Heliodorus, and called the *Aethiopica* (originally in a private
library, retrieved at the siege of Buda), that has been known in
Europe since it was printed at Basle in 1534.

In this story the queen of Ethiopia gives birth to a white
baby, and is afraid she will be accused of adultery. So she gives
the child—a daughter—into the care of the gymnosophists—
that is, the naked philosophers, who are hermits and mystics.
The girl, who is called Charicleia, is finally taken to Delphi,
where she becomes one of the priestesses of Artemis. There she
meets a noble Thessalian named Theagenes, who falls in love
with her and, with the help of a clever Egyptian, carries her off.
The Ethiopian queen, as it turns out, has never ceased to long
for her daughter and has hired this very Egyptian to search for
her. Mischance and adventures continue until all the main characters meet at Meroe, and Charicleia is rescued—again—just as
she is about to be sacrificed by her own father.

Interesting themes were thick as flies here, and the tale had a natural continuing fascination for Juliet. Particularly the part about the gymnosophists. She tried to find out as much as she could about these people, who were usually referred to as Hindu philosophers. Was India, in this case, presumed to be adjacent to Ethiopia? No—Heliodorus came late enough to know his geography better than that. The gymnosophists would be wanderers, far spread, attracting and repelling those they lived amongst with their ironclad devotion to purity of life and thought, their contempt for possessions, even for clothing and food. A beautiful maiden reared amongst them might well be left with some perverse hankering for a bare, ecstatic life.

Juliet had made a new friend named Larry. He taught Greek, and he had let Juliet store the garbage bags in the basement of his house. He liked to imagine how they might make the *Aethiopica* into a musical. Juliet collaborated in this fantasy, even to making up the marvellously silly songs and the preposterous stage effects. But she was secretly drawn to devising a different ending, one that would involve renunciation, and a backward search, in which the girl would be sure to meet fakes and charlatans, impostors, shabby imitations of what she was really looking for. Which was reconciliation, at last, with the erring, repentant, essentially great-hearted queen of Ethiopia.

Juliet was almost certain that she had seen Mother Shipton here in Vancouver. She had taken some clothes that she would never wear again (her wardrobe had grown increasingly utilitarian) to a Salvation Army Thrift Store, and as she set the bag down in the receiving room she saw a fat old woman in a muumuu fixing tags onto trousers. The woman was chatting with the other workers. She had the air of a supervisor, a cheerful but vigilant overseer—or perhaps the air of a woman who would assume that role whether she had any official superiority or not.

If she was in fact Mother Shipton, she had come down in the world. But not by very much. For if she was Mother Shipton, would she not have reserves of buoyancy and self-approbation, such as to make real downfall impossible?

Reserves of advice, pernicious advice, as well.

She has come to us here in great hunger.

Juliet had told Larry about Penelope. She had to have one person who knew. "Should I have talked to her about a noble life?" she said. "Sacrifice? Opening your life to the needs of strangers? I never thought of it. I must have acted as if it would have been good enough if she turned out like me. Would that sicken her?"

Larry was not a man who wanted anything from Juliet but her friendship and good humor. He was what used to be called an old-fashioned bachelor, asexual as far as she could tell (but probably she could not tell far enough), squeamish about any personal revelations, endlessly entertaining.

Two other men had appeared who wanted her as a partner. One of them she had met when he sat down at her sidewalk table. He was a recent widower. She liked him, but his loneliness was so raw and his pursuit of her so desperate that she became alarmed.

The other man was Christa's brother, whom she had met several times during Christa's life. His company suited her—in many ways he was like Christa. His marriage had ended long ago, he was not desperate—she knew, from Christa, that there had been women ready to marry him whom he had avoided. But he was too rational, his choice of her verged on being cold-blooded, there was something humiliating about it.

But why humiliating? It was not as if she loved him.

It was while she was still seeing Christa's brother—his name was Gary Lamb—that she ran into Heather, on a downtown street in Vancouver. Juliet and Gary had just come out of a theater where they had seen an early-evening movie, and they were talking about where to go for dinner. It was a warm night in summer, the light still not gone from the sky.

A woman detached herself from a group on the sidewalk. She came straight at Juliet. A thin woman, perhaps in her late thirties. Fashionable, with taffy streaks in her dark hair.

"Mrs. Porteous. Mrs. Porteous."

Juliet knew the voice, though she would never have known the face. Heather.

"This is incredible," Heather said. "I'm here for three days and I'm leaving tomorrow. My husband's at a conference. I was thinking that I don't know anybody here anymore and then I turn around and see you."

Juliet asked her where she was living now and she said Connecticut.

"And just about three weeks ago I was visiting Josh—you remember my brother Josh?—I was visiting my brother Josh and his family in Edmonton and I ran into Penelope. Just like this, on the street. No—actually it was in the mall, that humongous mall they have. She had a couple of her kids with her, she'd brought them down to get uniforms for that school they go to. The boys. We were both flabbergasted. I didn't know her right away but she recognized me. She'd flown down, of course. From that place way up north. But she says it's quite civilized, really. And she said you were still living here. But I'm with these people—they're my husband's friends—and I really haven't had time to ring you up—"

Juliet made some gesture to say that of course there would not be time and she had not expected to be rung up.

She asked how many children Heather had.

"Three. They're all monsters. I hope they grow up in a hurry. But my life's a picnic compared with Penelope's. *Five*."

"Yes."

"I have to run now, we're going to see a movie. I don't even know anything about it, I don't even like French movies. But it was altogether great meeting you like this. My mother and dad moved to White Rock. They used to see you all the time on TV. They used to brag to their friends that you'd lived in our house. They say you're not on anymore, did you get sick of it?"

"Something like that."

"I'm coming, I'm coming." She hugged and kissed Juliet, the way everybody did now, and ran to join her companions.

So. Penelope did not live in Edmonton—she had *come down* to Edmonton. Flown down. That meant she must live in Whitehorse or in Yellowknife. Where else was there that she could describe as *quite civilized*? Maybe she was being ironical, mocking Heather a bit, when she said that.

She had five children and two at least were boys. They were being outfitted with school uniforms. That meant a private school. That meant money.

Heather had not known her at first. Did that mean she had aged? That she was out of shape after five pregnancies, that she had not *taken care of herself*? As Heather had. As Juliet had, to a certain extent. That she was one of those women to whom the whole idea of such a struggle seemed ridiculous, a confession of insecurity? Or just something she had no time for—far outside of her consideration.

Juliet had thought of Penelope being involved with transcendentalists, of her having become a mystic, spending her life in contemplation. Or else—rather the opposite but still radically simple and spartan—earning her living in a rough and risky way, fishing, perhaps with a husband, perhaps also with some husky little children, in the cold waters of the Inside Passage off the British Columbia coast.

Not at all. She was living the life of a prosperous, practical matron. Married to a doctor, maybe, or to one of those civil servants managing the northern parts of the country during the time when their control is being gradually, cautiously, but with some fanfare, relinquished to the native people. If she ever met Penelope again they might laugh about how wrong Juliet had been. When they told about their separate meetings with Heather, how weird that was, they would laugh.

No. No. The fact was surely that she had already laughed too much around Penelope. Too many things had been jokes. Just as too many things—personal things, loves that were maybe just gratification—had been tragedies. She had been lacking in motherly inhibitions and propriety and self-control.

Penelope had said that she, Juliet, was still living in Vancouver. She had not told Heather anything about the breach. Surely not. If she had been told, Heather would not have spoken so easily.

How did Penelope know that she was still here, unless she checked in the phone directory? And if she did, what did that mean?

Nothing. Don't make it mean anything.

She walked to the curb to join Gary, who had tactfully moved away from the scene of the reunion.

Whitehorse, Yellowknife. It was painful indeed to know the names of those places—places she could fly to. Places where she could loiter in the streets, devise plans for catching glimpses.

But she was not so mad. She must not be so mad.

At dinner, she thought that the news she had just absorbed put her into a better situation for marrying Gary, or living with him—whatever it was he wanted. There was nothing to worry about, or hold herself in wait for, concerning Penelope. Penelope was not a phantom, she was safe, as far as anybody is safe, and she was probably as happy as anybody is happy. She had detached herself from Juliet and very likely from the memory of Juliet, and Juliet could not do better than to detach herself in turn.

But she had told Heather that Juliet was living in Vancouver. Did she say *Juliet?* Or *Mother. My mother.*

Juliet told Gary that Heather was the child of old friends. She had never spoken to him about Penelope, and he had never given any sign of knowing about Penelope's existence. It was possible that Christa had told him, and he had remained silent out of a consideration that it was none of his business. Or that Christa had told him, and he had forgotten. Or that Christa had never mentioned anything about Penelope, not even her name.

If Juliet lived with him the fact of Penelope would never surface, Penelope would not exist.

Nor did Penelope exist. The Penelope Juliet sought was gone. The woman Heather had spotted in Edmonton, the mother who had brought her sons to Edmonton to get their school uniforms, who had changed in face and body so that Heather did not recognize her, was nobody Juliet knew.

Does Juliet believe this?

If Gary saw that she was agitated he pretended not to notice. But it was probably on this evening that they both understood they would never be together. If it had been possible for them to be together she might have said to him, *My daughter went away without telling me good-bye and in fact she probably did not know then that she was going. She did not know it was for good. Then gradually, I believe, it dawned on her how much she wanted to stay away. It is just a way that she has found to manage her life.*

"It's maybe the explaining to me that she can't face. Or has not *time for, really. You know, we always have the idea that there is this reason or that reason and we keep trying to find out reasons. And I could tell you plenty about what I've done wrong. But I think the reason may be something not so easily dug out. Something like purity in her nature. Yes. Some fineness and strictness and purity, some rock-hard honesty in her. My father used to say of someone he disliked, that he had no use for that person. Couldn't those words mean simply what they say? Penelope does not have a use for me.*

Maybe she can't stand me. It's possible.

Juliet has friends. Not so many now—but friends. Larry continues to visit, and to make jokes. She keeps on with her studies. The word *studies* does not seem to describe very well what she does—*investigations* would be better.

And being short of money, she works some hours a week at the coffee place where she used to spend so much time at the sidewalk tables. She finds this work a good balance for her involvement with the old Greeks—so much so that she believes she wouldn't quit even if she could afford to.

She keeps on hoping for a word from Penelope, but not in any strenuous way. She hopes as people who know better hope for undeserved blessings, spontaneous remissions, things of that sort.

Andrea

1044734805

506 2750664